MUTANT CITY BLUES

HARD HELIX
BY
ROBIN D LAWS

HARD HELIX

CREDITS

Publisher: Simon Rogers

Author: Robin D Laws

Art: Cover and some interior art Jérôme Huguenin, other interior art Pascal Quidault

Layout: Roderick Robertson, based on a design by Jérôme Huguenin

Playtesters: Nick Wedig, Adam Davis, Neel Krishnaswami, Amber Wedig, Neil Ford and group, Mike Grace, Anthony Sweeting, Kev Hickman, Zane Goodin, Chuk Goodin, Gordon Wilson, Robert Miller, Jennifer Miller, Anne Freitas, Kelly Warner, Roger Clark, Patrick Sweeney

© 2009 Pelgrane Press Ltd. All Rights Reserved.

Mutant City Blues is a trademark of Pelgrane Press Ltd.

CONTENTS

WHAT'S IN THIS BOOK   4

THE HARD HELIX   5

    Backstory   5
    The Crime   5
    The Suspects   5
    The Twist   5
    The Culprit   5
    Scenes   5
    The Crime Scene   5
    Interviews and Interrogations   8
    Information Gathering   16
    Action   18
    Drama   19
    Wrap-Up   19

THE VANISHERS   21

    Backstory   21
    The Crime   21
    The Investigation   21
    The Twist   21
    The Culprits   21
    Scenes   21
    A Frantic Call   21
    Four Punks and a Patsy   22
    Criminal Mastermind   24
    Broadway Bob   25
    Bob's Bookmaker   26
    Coffin On Wheels   26
    Hijacking Ring   28
    A Long-Term Case   28
    The Vetroni Outfit   29
    Jason "the Machine" Vetroni   30
    Paul "The Lawyer" Martelli   31
    Danny "Flipper" De Filippo   31
    Al "Popper" Soldati   32
    Salvatore "Boom Boom" Spiggia   32
    Peter "Snakes" Guidelli   33
    John Carboni   33
    Takedown   35
    Conducting Interviews   35
    A Big Finish?   36

SUPER SQUAD   38

    Backstory   38
    The Crime   38
    The Investigation   38
    The Twist   38
    The Culprit   39
    Scenes   39
    Riot In Helixtown   39
    Beamed Out   41
    Canvassing the Rioters   42
    The Sad Apartment Of Irwin Poling   45
    The Neighbor   46
    Eating Cheese With the Rat Squad   47
    Drive-By   48
    No Snitching   50
    Hunting Lamar   51
    Mourning Lamar   52
    Ease Off   52
    Up In Smoke   52
    The Big Skate   54
    Chain Of Custody   54
    The Locker   55
    Michelle Cracks   56
    Showdown   57
    Wrap-Up   58

CELL DIVISION   60

    Backstory   60
    The Crime   60
    The Investigation   60
    The Twist   60
    The Culprit   60
    Scenes   60
    Lucky Shoes   60
    Super Siege   61
    Chillingly Fanatical   63
    Background Checks   64
    Mutant Manifesto   66
    The Big Bulletin   66
    Death On the Tracks   68
    Tracing the Call   69
    Hunting Milan   69
    Super Pox   70
    Container SY-7   70
    Trailing Gaines   71
    Faces Of Terror   72
    Ringleader   74
    Wrap-Up   75

INVESTIGATIVE ABILITY CHECKLIST   77

WHAT'S IN THIS BOOK

Hard Helix contains four scenarios for Mutant City Blues, the GUMSHOE game of police investigation in a mutant-powered world. Like any scenario collection, it's for GM eyes only.

Cases contained in this book are:

The Hard Helix: This scenario introduces the major players of Mutant City and revolves around the central mystery of the Sudden Mutation Event. It emphasizes clue-gathering and interrogation room savvy over super powered action. The scenario's many entry points into the political ecology of the city and the mutant rights movement make it an ideal follow-up to the sample adventure in the Mutant City Blues rulebook.

The Vanishers: The squad's intervention in a jewelry store robbery leads them into an operation against the new school, mutant-bolstered forces of organized crime. A brief investigation leads to an open-ended case in which squad members must devise and execute a long-term strategy to bring down an emergent mob family.

Super Squad: A sudden death at a mutant-related riot leads the unit into the twisted world of the Super Squad, an elite policing group who work the city's toughest streets—and have, in the process, gotten more than a little dirty. Squads struck by the typical roleplaying impulse to set aside the rulebook may hew closer to the straight and narrow after seeing where police corruption leads.

Cell Division: The detectives confront a homegrown terrorist threat from a previously unknown group of mutant supremacists. Can they uncover the truth behind the Mutant Revolutionary Front — one that remains shrouded even from its own suicidally indoctrinated followers? This scenario provides a mix of investigation and action.

THE HARD HELIX

This introductory adventure introduces the players to many of Mutant City's key figures, and reinforces the central mystery of the SME.

BACKSTORY

Controversial scholar of anamorphology Sidney Dorris is found murdered the evening before his scheduled announcement of an explanation for SME. What was his secret, and who was willing to kill him for it?

THE CRIME

Dorris is found his luxury hotel room, where he was staying as an attendee of the Quade Institute's annual Symposium On Anamorphological Research (SOAR), dead from multiple gunshot wounds.

THE SUSPECTS

Lucius Quade, father of anamorphology, who considered the attention-seeking Dorris a threat to the discipline.

Anti-mutant activist Conrad Priestley, who feared Dorris' discovery would further legitimate the gene-expressive community.

City councillor Brian Schmiederer, who lost funding for a community project due to Dorris' financial shenanigans.

Billionaire mutant Galen Birch, who Dorris swindled.

Former research assistant Crystal Flores, who he sexually harassed and professionally exploited

Certified paranoid Chip Silver, whose research Dorris plagiarized.

Ava Singleton, with whom Dorris was having an affair.

THE TWIST

The detectives discover that Dorris was a mutant, gifted with Kinetic Energy Dispersal. This begs the question: how do you shoot a bulletproof man?

THE CULPRIT

Dorris died because he deliberately turned off his power when he saw who was trying to kill him: his long-suffering wife Gloria, distraught over her discovery that Dorris had impregnated his mistress.

SCENES

After the crime scene, which for obvious reasons has to be the first scene, possible sequences can mostly be played out in an order dictated by player choices.

Items of information appearing under the same ability, but separated by bullet-points, can be split up between different characters using the same ability. If only one PC on the scene has that ability, they can glean all of these separated clues.

THE CRIME SCENE

SCENE TYPE: PHYSICAL EVIDENCE

"The Hard Helix" begins *in media res*, with the detectives entering the crime scene, having been assigned the case by their watch commander. It presumes that the PCs have been active as HCIU detectives for a while. They know each other, and are well acquainted with the demands of the job.

(Alternately, if this is your first episode, you can start by asking each of the players to describe a brief scene establishing their characters, at the end of which they get the call to head over to the hotel.)

This scene is set in a swanky hotel in your chosen city. Uniformed officers are already present. Medical

HARD HELIX

examiner Mads Jensen (See *Mutant City Blues* p. 149) is there to deliver preliminary findings from a cursory look at the body. He has his gloves on, ready to begin the examination, after photographs are taken and the lead detective on the case gives him the word. Police photographer Lucy Bellaver is already snapping away. Criminalist Ed "the Ted" Riley (See *Mutant City Blues* p. 150) is there too, ready to bag and tag physical evidence as requested by the team. "Dudes," Riley intones, by way of greeting, "this guy is some big cheese."

Dorris lies dead on his back. Three small red bullet holes pierce the starched fabric of his white dress shirt. A large pool of blood stains the expensive broadloom around him. He's also clad in black dress slacks and dark socks. An untied bow tie is still wrapped around his collar. The cuffs of his shirt are unfastened; gold cuff links sit in their velvet-lined case on top of the hotel's desk. The room's curtains are closed.

Hotel manager Harry Fields hovers outside the room, waiting to answer questions, as does Isabel Gameros, the housecleaning staffer who found his body.

The following information is available in this scene.

Talking to Ed "the Ted": The victim is Sidney Dorris, a famous anamorphologist. He was in town for SOAR, annual Symposium On Anamorphological Research, sponsored by the Quade Institute. He was all over the media because he was due, in a couple of hours, to address assembled scholars and scientists with a much-heralded explanation for the SME. Dorris is famous as a gadfly, and thorn in Lucius Quade's side. *Ted volunteers all of this information in one burst, if prompted to expand on his "big cheese" comment.*

Talking to Isabel: Isabel wants to cooperate but is nervous and has a shaky command of English. She provides the following information only in response to specific questions, answering as briefly as she can. She opened the door about ninety minutes ago, just after 10 AM, to clean the room.

There was no "Do Not Disturb" sign on the door.

She used the phone in the room to call the front desk and let them know that they had a murdered guest on their hands. Other than that, she didn't touch or move anything.

Harry Fields arrived a few minutes later.

Isabel had no interaction with Mr. Dorris, except to clean his room when he was absent.

She doesn't snoop into, or keep track of, guests' possessions and can't say if anything has gone missing.

Talking to Harry (who waits for questions before volunteering information): When the front desk paged him with news of Isabel's call, he instructed them to contact 911, and came immediately to the room.

There are no security cameras in the hotel corridors.

The event Dorris was dressing for would presumably be the SOAR dinner and dance, which the hotel has hosted since its inception.

The dinner began at 7 PM.

The hotel's card-swipe system keeps track of each time a key card is used to open a door. The last time Dorris' room was unlocked from the outside—aside from Isabel's entry this morning—was at 3:43 PM yesterday.

The system can't tell when the door is opened from the inside.

The rooms on this floor are from a block reserved for SOAR.

Dorris paid for two occupants, but only one key card has been issued on the room.

Forensic Anthropology (or ask Mads): The bullet hits on his chest and abdomen are entry wounds.

They seem like those of a small caliber weapon, probably a .22 caliber.

There are only two exit wounds on Dorris' back. This is not surprising; .22s lose kinetic energy quickly and tend to move around in the body, bouncing off bones until finally coming to a rest in soft tissue.

Taking into account the chilly setting of the air conditioning, which has somewhat retarded decomposition, Dorris has been dead for sixteen to eighteen hours. This would put the time of death between 5:30 and 7:30 PM, give or take.

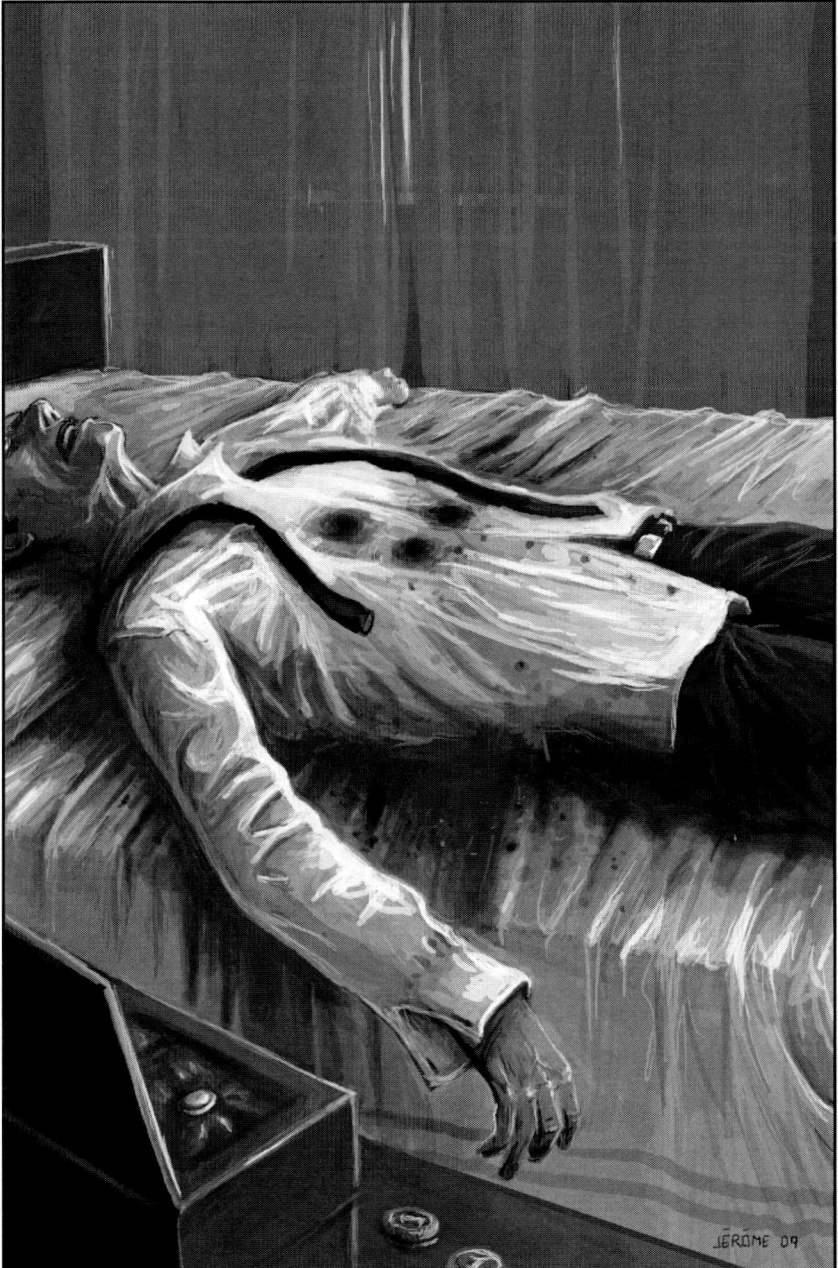

Evidence Collection: Two bullets lie below the room's window.

Ballistics: (after finding these bullets) These are .22 caliber bullets, both deformed by impact with the victim, and perhaps by secondary impacts with the objects that stopped them.

Evidence Collection: A dent in the metal radiator/air conditioner unit below the window seems to be a bullet hit.

(1 point spend) A hairline fracture in the window indicates that the bullet hit the curtains, further reducing their kinetic energy, so that the bullet cracked, but did not exit through, its thick glass.

A fourth bullet lies under an armchair. (This numbering makes the correct assumption that the third bullet is still in Dorris' abdomen.)

Ballistics: (after finding the fourth bullet) It is a .22 caliber, matching the two found below the window.

It was fired but is otherwise in pristine condition, as if it didn't hit anything at all—not a person, not a wall or other object.

There are no holes in the chair, so, to be where it was discovered, the fourth bullet would to have been somehow moved after being fired.

Data Retrieval: Dorris' laptop sits on the desk. Its hard drive has been removed. There's a CD in the drive, but it's only a DVD of a recent movie.

Fingerprinting: (Timed Result, after lab work) Dorris' prints appear on the laptop's screen and keys, but there are no other prints around the removed hard drive.

1-point spend: This does not necessarily indicate that the perp took any special precautions against fingerprinting; the matte plastic surface of this area of the keyboard is not a particularly good medium for useful prints.

Evidence Collection: No notes or scientific papers can be found in the room. Dorris' briefcase is present, and there's an empty folder inside, but no copy of his speech, no papers, no notebook, no PDA device, no nothing.

Dorris' cell phone sits on the floor, plugged into the socket to recharge. He files all of his contacts by first name, so there's no apparent next of kin to call.

HARD HELIX

CANVASSING HOTEL GUESTS

An immediate canvass of the nearby rooms finds few guests currently present. (Most of them are at the Quade Institute, attending the symposium.) The detectives find only a few people still in their rooms.

Dr. Mala Gowariker, heads the anamorphology department of the University of Delhi, India, specializing in SEDS research. Mala tries to brush off the detectives. She's impatient to get going because she doesn't want to miss Dorris' presentation at the Institute. When she hears he's dead, she's taken aback but not visibly upset. (Like certain other brilliant scientists, her sense of empathy isn't as sharp as it might be.) After hearing the news, she becomes willing to talk. She's mostly concerned about the fate of his presentation. Will somebody be able to reconstruct it from his notes? Did his PowerPoint presentation include enough of an audio component to be comprehensible without an accompanying speech?

If asked who might have done it, Mala blithely assumes that it was one of her colleagues. "He was a very boastful, irritating man. He had a way of making you want to kill him." If pressed for names of possible suspects, Mala says she's joking and indicates that prominent anamorphologists are frequently harassed by anti-mutant activists. If asked to name Dorris' main professional rivals, she mentions Lucius Quade himself, and his former assistant, Crystal Flores.

Dorris used to be Quade's right hand man but broke with him about five years ago. He's now affiliated with the University of ###. ### is a large university within driving distance of Mutant City. (Or, in Europe, within a day's travel by train.)

He was a brilliant thinker but his recent work was erratic and much-disputed. His presentation on the origins of the SME was supposed to be his comeback. It either would have restored him in the anamorphological pecking order, or made him a laughing-stock forever.

She left for the ballroom area at about 6 PM, along with many other colleagues. The dinner provides a major occasion for networking, and nearly everybody goes early to mill around in the hallways and chat. Since all nearby rooms were booked by SOAR, it's unsurprising if no one was present to hear the shots ring out.

(Other anamorphologists can convey the same information, although perhaps not so bluntly.)

Vernetta Brown is an lecturer in anamorphology from Regent University in Virginia. She'd never met Dorris but was looking forward to his presentation with great interest. Like Dr. Gowariker, she was down at the informal pre-dinner reception during the apparent time of the murder. Regent is an avowedly Christian institution founded by the evangelist Pat Robertson. Brown is not a scientist but a theologian. She belongs to a movement hoping to find the Biblical roots of the SME—that is, to either credit God for it, or blame it on the devil. She was hopeful that Dorris' evidence would advance her own studies.

Milton Gaines, a freelance writer, is covering SOAR for *The New Scientist* magazine. Gaines is a frail, elderly man suffering from noticeable tremors. **Forensic Anthropology** reveals that he probably suffers from Parkinson's disease. When first questioned, Gaines says he heard nothing, and that he went down to the dinner around 6 PM. **Bullshit Detector** suggests that he's hiding something. In fact, he skipped the dinner because he was feeling unwell. (This can be determined conclusively by checking his account at the hotel; he ordered room service at about 8:15 PM. A detective will have to use a suitable interpersonal ability on Harry Fields or another hotel staffer to gain access to this confidential information. Fields responds to **Intimidation** or **Negotiation**. Other staff might allow access after **Flattery** or **Flirting**.) Gaines did hear shots ring out but is feeling guilty and ashamed that he was too frightened to do anything or alert anyone about them. He fears that his seeming cowardice will jeopardize his reputation as a writer. **Reassurance** convinces him that the detectives will treat this understandable lapse with discretion. He then admits that he heard four shots ring out at approximately 7:15 PM. First one, then a pause, then another three in rapid succession. He knows they were gunshots because, back when he was a much healthier and braver man, he was a war correspondent. Frightened, he remained in his room, and didn't dare to look to see anyone leaving the room afterwards. He didn't hear footsteps, so the person probably went in the opposite direction.

INTERVIEWS AND INTERROGATIONS

The opportunity for a first interview with Gloria Dorris comes at the PCs unexpectedly. They dictate the order of other interviews—although some suspects will appear on their list only after speaking to others.

GLORIA DORRIS

As the detectives are finishing up at the hotel (or during a suitable lull in the action) Harry Fields approaches them, an anxious look on his face. Dorris' wife, Gloria, has just arrived. She's at the front desk, asking for her room key.

This gives the PCs the unwelcome task of informing Gloria that her husband has been killed. Her explosive grief when they inform her is genuine and interferes with the unit's **Bullshit Detectors**, making everything she says seem honest.

Gloria demands to see her husband and becomes nearly hysterical if prevented from doing so, to the point of trying to push past the detectives and head up to the room herself. She already knows the room number from speaking to Sidney (and, of course, from killing him there.) **Reassurance** will calm her down, but she remains intent on seeing the body right away. A 2-point spend gets her to relent on this demand entirely.

In response to specific questioning, she provides the following information. To help keep the story straight in your head, false statements are given in italics.

Gloria traveled later than Sidney *because she had a deadline to meet before she left*; she works as a graphic designer. Gloria drove to Mutant City unaccompanied.

(In truth, she arrived separately, but on the same day as Sidney, in an attempt to catch him in the arms of his assistant/mistress, Ava Singleton. The deadline story is one she told Dorris, too. Gloria stayed at a less expensive hotel within walking distance of this one.)

At the time of the killing, she was at home in another city, uploading a file to a client. If the detectives need confirmation of this, a check of the time stamp on her client's server will confirm this. (She set up her computer to automate this task. At the time, she was creating an alibi only for Sidney's benefit, in case he accused her of snooping on him. This isn't the first time she's gone to a conference to see if he's sleeping with an assistant.)

Sidney was not, as far as she knew, a mutant.

Like all top anamorphologists, Sidney was regularly threatened by anti-mutant activists. *The killer must have been one of them.* Threats increased after he announced he'd found the cause of the SME. They seemed to fear that, whatever it was, it would make mutants seem less freakish to the general population.

After answering the above question, she asks if Sidney's lecture materials have been recovered. She knows they haven't, because she took them, and is trying to point the detectives toward a red herring.

During a phone conversation (conducted by cell on both sides), Sidney reported a nasty confrontation with a horrible anti-mutant type, who smelled like cat pee. (**Trivia** says that this can only describe the local leader of the NPL, Conrad Priestley.)

Sidney was a difficult man, and their marriage had its ups and downs. But through it all, she never stopped loving him. On a 1-point **Reassurance** or **Intimidation** spend, she'll spell out what this means: she knew that Sidney was "occasionally" unfaithful to her. If asked if she had an arrangement with Sidney, or an open marriage, she, with a sense of quiet anger, denies it. (In other words, Sidney merely acted as if they had arrangement.)

She and Sidney are childless.

He feared that the distractions of fatherhood would prevent him from making the scientific breakthroughs he owed the world. Although she wanted to have kids, she accepted this as a condition of remaining with him.

(core) Sidney's assistant, Ava Singleton, will need to be told of this. She's attending the conference, but is probably not staying at this costly hotel. (Gloria provides her cell phone number.)

Ava is a nice kid, though Gloria admits she wasn't always that nice to her, *probably because she saw her as a symbol of her husband's workaholism*.

Sidney and Lucius Quade were barely on speaking terms. Lucius tried to keep Sidney in his shadow, and resented his leaving the Institute. (This isn't really the case, but Sidney believed it, and convinced Gloria it was true also.)

Gloria has no idea what Sidney's big theory about the SME was, and couldn't care less. (If she did care, she could have checked his hard drive or papers to find out what it was, but has already destroyed this incriminating evidence by dropping a duffle bag containing the papers and smashed hard drive into the nearest large body of water.)

LUCIUS QUADE

Lucius Quade is described in *Mutant City Blues*, p. 141. His response to news of Dorris' death, if the detectives are the first to inform him of it, is to quietly shake his head. He asks immediately if they have a suspect. If he senses that the detectives consider him a suspect, he's taken aback and asks them if he should be speaking to a lawyer first. Quade is an important man and expects deference from public officials, especially mutant ones. He bristles visibly if questioned harshly, but, as man with nothing to hide, continues to respond honestly. He'll provide the following information in response to suitably specific questions.

At the time of the killing, Quade was stuck in traffic, on the way from the Institute. There was no one in the car with him. He was letting his cell phone calls go to voicemail as he reviewed the remarks he was scheduled to make at the banquet.

Yes, there was bad blood between himself and Sidney Dorris. Dorris was too much of a one-man show to survive at the Quade Institute, which demands team players.

In his opinion, Dorris needed the supervision of skeptical colleagues. His later work grew increasingly sloppy. He wrote a couple of popular best sellers and made his presence felt on the talk circuit, but never made the major breakthrough he seemed to think himself destined for.

Quade opposed the move to give Dorris a platform without knowing how credible his theory would be. But he's only one member of the symposium board, and was overruled by others. Maybe they were right—registrations for this year's event are up by 23%.

(core) Quade was looking forward to the banquet, because he'd arranged to sit Dorris next to Galen Birch, who Dorris once swindled out of a five-figure sum.

If Dorris was in contact with Conrad Priestley, it was more likely to cook up some publicity stunt together. (This is Quade's honestly held but untrue and uncharitable opinion.)

When he got tipsy, Dorris would sometimes hint that he was a closeted mutant. Quade finds it hard to believe that, if he could fly or read minds, that he wouldn't have boasted about it constantly. But with him, you could never tell what was real, and what was typical Sidney BS.

CONRAD PRIESTLEY

Conrad Priestley (*Mutant City Blues* p.151) is sullen and unresponsive when confronted with heightened detectives. He prefers to pepper them with anti-mutant insults. **Intimidation** prompts him to grudgingly answer their questions—though not without the occasional segue into slurs and abuse.

As a famous advocate of mutant rights, Dorris was a menace to the pure community second only to the genetic traitor Lucius Quade. Whoever shot him did a favor to mankind. Not that the NPL *condones* that sort of thing, mind you…

Yes, Priestley did confront Dorris the night before the murder, in an NPL picket line of the SOAR opening ceremonies. SOAR is nothing but a massive propaganda campaign to legitimize the mongrelization of the human bloodline, and as such must be opposed by anyone concerned for the future of the species. Conrad singled out Dorris for a good spitting on because he recognized him from his television appearances.

Dorris was insolently cocky in the face of Priestley's righteous vituperation, wiping the spit from his face and inviting Priestley to have coffee with him. Conrad went, curious to see what corrupt truths the devil would attempt to whisper in his ear.

His conversation with Dorris was baffling. Conrad expected an argument for mutant rights, but instead Dorris kept pressing him about something called the Cube Project, which he was supposed to know something about due to his alleged connection to the Aryan Nations.

A character with **Anthropology** can explain the odd connection between the NPL and the Aryans. They do share a network of connections, and many NPLers were straight-up racists before the SME. Although some of them continue to socialize, especially behind bars, each group thinks that the other has grown w79eak and tolerant—the NPL, because it accepts pures of all races and religious faiths, and the Aryans, because they allow mutants to join them, so long as they're reliably Caucasian.

History places the Cube Project as an all-purpose conspiracy theory, explaining everything from Zionist domination to cattle mutilations. The theory has shown an almost mythic elasticity; various groups interpret it according to their own agendas. (1-point spend): the version of the theory most popular among the far right describes it as an attempt by the US government to infiltrate possible feeder groups for domestic terror cells, including the Aryan Nations.

When it became clear that Priestley could tell him nothing about it, Dorris rudely and dismissively departed—without even paying for Conrad's coffee. That was the last Priestley ever saw of him.

(core) If anyone had reason to have Dorris shanked, it would be that freak councillor, Brian Schmiederer. It was Dorris' financial improprieties that sank Schmiederer's effort to establish a propaganda machine to brainwash the city's children, thank the Lord. You'd need to look for a contract hire, though, because the little weasel wouldn't dare get his hands dirty.

Conrad was out helping his elderly mother shop for groceries at the time of Dorris' death, and nowhere near the hotel.

This last statement lights up the group's **Bullshit Detectors**.

If interviewed, Conrad's dear old mother, Magda, at first attempts to alibi her son, but quickly crumbles if offered, through **Flattery**, any positive attention. Compliments for her somewhat stale jam cookies are especially welcome. She says that poor Conrad's memory must be going: he helped her with her shopping two days ago, not one. (Magda does not live with Conrad; she's allergic to his many cats. On a 1-point **Forensic Psychology** spend, a character contemplating this concludes that this may be why Conrad has filled his apartment with nearly a dozen of the little beasts.)

Data Retrieval, when used to study surveillance tapes from the hotel exterior and lobby around the killing, reveals Priestley's statement to be a lie. Conrad Priestley is seen along with several young barhead allies, attempting to enter the hotel's ballroom area. He is then rebuffed by guards from Petula Security. They are carrying a large and somewhat suspicious duffle bag.

If confronted with the footage—or if he begins to fear he's being fingered for Dorris' murder, Priestley cops to an abortive attempt to sabotage the SOAR dinner with a massive stinkbomb. "It was legitimate civil disobedience," he claims.

BRIAN SCHMIEDERER

Councillor Schmiederer (*Mutant City Blues* p. 145) remains forthcoming and friendly with detectives even if he realizes that he's been named as an enemy of the murder victim. He becomes upset only if it becomes clear that they've come after him on Conrad Priestley's recommendation. After this bomb drops, a credibly mollifying use of **Bureaucracy**, **Flattery**, **Negotiation** or **Reassurance** is needed to keep him talking. Otherwise, he refers all further inquiries to his private attorney.

His answers to specific questions are as follows:

At the time of the killing, Brian was down in the lobby of the hotel, as the many worthies of the mutant community and anamorphological discipline he was glad-handing can attest.

When Dorris was still a star of the Quade Institute, he served as a chairman on a dream project of Schmiederer's—a Museum of the Evolving Helix, to be built in Brian's ward. This would be a hands-on science museum aimed especially at the young, to educate them on genetics and biotech in general, and particularly on the challenges facing the mutant community. The project was already a tough sell. Then it was revealed that Dorris was charging personal expenses, including champagne, flowers, high-end chocolate and expensive lingerie, to the foundation's account. The project has been on hold ever since—with Dorris skipping town shortly thereafter.

(core) From the nature of the items Dorris charged to the project, it was pretty clear that the he was having an affair and keeping the financial traces out of his wife's sight. Brian wasn't sure who Sidney was sleeping with, but he seemed awfully familiar with his pretty assistant, Crystal Flores.

Brian was hoping that Dorris would fall completely on his face with that presentation of his, but would never in a million years commission a murder. Never!

GALEN BIRCH

The world's richest mutant (*Mutant City Blues* p. 142) is only too happy to talk to the cops—provided that they seem to be primarily interested in gathering dirt on the deceased, against whom he bore a considerable

HARD HELIX

grudge. He becomes spooked if the detectives come at him too hard or seem to regard him as a suspect. If that happens, they'll have to pivot quickly to schmooze him back into cooperation. Otherwise, he directs all inquiries to his formidable phalanx of high-priced legal talent. Given Birch's mammoth ego, **Flattery** is always a reliable bet, but he'll also respond to **Flirting** (from attractive female detectives), **Negotiation**, or **Reassurance**.

He volunteers the following information, whether asked or not:

Dorris was a persuasive con artist, who swindled him out of nearly half a million dollars. This isn't the first time Sidney announced a breakthrough explanation for the SME. Five years ago, he came to Birch and promised just such a revelation if Birch's Whiteoak Foundation would underwrite his research. Birch squandered the research funds, diverting much of the money into his own pocket. This went on for several years until Birch demanded a full accounting, including Dorris' results to date—and got nothing in return.

Birch provides this information in response to suitably specific questions:

Birch arrived at the SOAR dinner late, having been delayed by "a business issue." If aggressively pressed, he explains that a hedge fund he was heavily invested in had just taken a sizeable hit, and he needed to take time out to "discuss strategy with" (read: scream at) its manager.

Although he could certainly afford it, and has plenty of connections of that nature from his time heading Betula Security Consultants, Birch would never have an enemy whacked. He had much worse plans for Dorris—he was going to sic his lawyers on him, demanding full rights to any proceeds from his most current SME theory. (If the detectives have given him any reason to believe that their ethics are malleable, Birch will then hint that he'll make it worth their while to give him advance or exclusive access to Dorris' SME notes, if they should recover them.)

If asked what Dorris' original SME theory was, Birch says he's embarrassed to talk about it now, and only speaks if the detectives agree to keep it on the Q.T. Dorris came to him claiming that he'd found an unusual electromagnetic emanation coming out of the Bermuda Triangle at the exact time of the

earliest SME symptoms. Birch subsequently had this checked out by reputable scholars, who thoroughly debunked it. Dorris' theories not only referenced the wackiest of paranormal claims, but were based on inaccurate technical readings. There was no spike in electromagnetic activity anywhere that day, and much less in the Bermuda Triangle. But Dorris had a convincing way about him that could make anyone—particularly a scientific layman like Birch—want to believe him.

(core) Although Dorris professed not to be a mutant himself, Birch found out otherwise, when he hired private detectives to engage in a belated background check. If the detectives made an appointment in advance, Birch has a DVD to show them. If they surprise him, he supplies it later, making it a Timed Result clue. The DVD contains surreptitiously-taken video footage of Dorris performing repair work on his vintage Ferrari. He's under the car when he discovers that he needs a tool sitting several meters away. His arm elongates, snakes out, snatches the wrench, and zips back into place. **Anamorphology** identifies this as a clear use of the Limb Extension power.

Dorris had an eye for the ladies. It was, in Birch's eyes, his only humanizing quality. (**Trivia** reminds an investigator of Birch's own adventures in serial monogamy.) As much as he hated Dorris, Birch considers a shot at the man's romantic activities to be hitting below the belt, and must be pressed to reveal that the man specialized in "banging his assistants."

CRYSTAL FLORES

A check of the symposium guest registry confirms that Dorris' ex-assistant, Crystal Flores, is an attendee. In her current capacity as adjunct professor of anamorphology at the University Of Texas A&M, she's scheduled to present her paper, *Vitamin Absorption In Adolescent Category-B Mutants: A Random Controlled Study* tomorrow at the Quade Institute. The schedule shows that this talk is booked into a small seminar hall, and would have conflicted with Dorris' much-anticipated presentation in the main lecture theater. Flores is staying at the hotel.

Flores is a twitchy, nervous presence, who eschews makeup, lets her eyebrows grow out, and wears her tangled hair in a severe knot. A character with the **Flirting** ability can tell that she's doing her best to disguise her natural beauty, presumably to deflect unwanted romantic attention. (**Research** turns up images of her from her days with Dorris, when her look was overtly glamorous.) Any detective trying to use **Flirting** to get information from her is immediately shut down; she looks past him as if he isn't there.

Crystal is extremely reluctant to talk about Sidney Dorris, saying that it's a chapter of her life she'd prefer not to revisit. She talks if the PCs use **Intimidation** to remind her that she's a prime suspect in a murder investigation.

She remains unforthcoming, giving only the minimum information called for by the team's specific questions:

She was Dorris' research assistant for two years, during the end of his tenure at the Quade Institute, and during his involvement with Brian Schmiederer's Museum of the Evolving Helix.

For the last year of that time, she was having an affair with him. It was a terrible mistake, one that has haunted her career ever since.

Dorris only takes pretty women as assistants. Ever afterwards, they'll be known as the fools who slept with him. Ironically, though, it's his early assistants, including her, who did all of his groundbreaking work for him.

Since leaving the Quade Institute, he's gone increasingly off the rails, pursuing a series of ever-crazier theories. He'd be better off going back to taking credit for his assistants' work.

It began as sexual harassment, but eventually she gave into his charms.

She had no idea that he was financing their romantic weekends with money swindled from the museum board.

(core) He told her that he and his wife had an arrangement, and that Gloria was okay with his extra-curricular activities as long as he used protection. She didn't believe this until one day when she phoned Dorris at his home and Gloria answered. She referred to their affair in an off-hand manner that suggested she knew about this, and accepted it, at least grudgingly.

Crystal was in her room at the time of Dorris' murder. She planned to skip the dinner entirely, for fear of running into him.

She'd never shoot Dorris. That would be an admission that he still had power over her.

If asked to suggest a likely suspect, Crystal says: "He's probably harassing his current assistant. And if I were you, I'd mark it down as justifiable homicide."

AVA SINGLETON

Ava is a blond woman in her late twenties with very fair skin who dresses in oversized sweaters and unflattering jeans. Obviously extremely distraught by Dorris' death, she cries throughout any interview with the detectives. **Reassurance** gets her to talk. A 2-point **Reassurance** spend gets her through the interview without breaking down. Otherwise, she'll be able to answer about five questions before losing it completely so that the detectives have to come back the next day to complete the interview.

HARD HELIX

A character with **Anamorphology** who engages her in conversation about the field discovers that her familiarity with it is that of an inattentive undergrad.

Without the 2-point Reassurance spend, she keeps her answers as brief as she can, because she's busy sobbing. With it, she'll be more expansive.

She denies having an affair with Dorris. **Bullshit Detector** reveals this as patently deceptive. **Intimidation** gets her to admit it.

She says that their affair was consensual from the first. "In fact, I pursued him."

Ava didn't stay with Dorris in his hotel room, because he'd be sharing it with his wife. She had a room at a cheaper hotel.

She didn't plan on attending the dinner, because it was hard for her to see Sidney and Gloria together.

As far as she knew, Gloria was running late but was supposed to make it to town in time for the dinner. But then she wasn't exactly up to date on the wife's comings and goings.

According to Sidney, he and his wife had an understanding. Their relationship was loveless, but he kept it up due to an unspecified mental illness on her part. (This is untrue, but it's Dorris' lie, which Ava believes.)

Ava's expertise is in History, specifically that of post-Cold War western intelligence agencies.

Dorris sought her out because he'd become convinced that the SME was the result, intentional or otherwise, of a black operation by the CIA or another intelligence agency.

He came increasingly to rely on a source he codenamed Platinum.

Lately, this Platinum had turned on him and began to call him around the clock. He got ahold of her number and harassed her, too. He claimed that Dorris had stolen his research, and was going to pay for it.

The threats began two weeks ago, at about the same time news of Dorris' impending announcement began to garner widespread media coverage.

(core) She captured Platinum's number on her cell phone but never called it. As his threats grew worse, she repeatedly urged Sidney to involve the police, but he wouldn't hear of it. Ava provides the number—it's local to Mutant City.

If a player asks to use **Forensic Psychology** for insights into Ava, say that she appears distracted above and beyond her obvious grief. On a 2-point **Forensic Anthropology** spend, a detective spots the signs of pregnancy. Ava is in the last weeks of her first trimester and has been able to conceal her condition by wearing baggy tops. (This is redundant, of course, if they have already learned about Ava's pregnancy from Chip Silver.)

CHIP SILVER

Chip Silver is a lifelong conspiracy theorist who lives in his mother's basement in a slightly rundown working class residential neighborhood. **Research** locates his home address from his cell phone number. Chip works for an onsite computer repair company and so is constantly on the move during business hours.

His mother Cloris is home during the day. She is very protective of Chip and does her best to discourage anyone from bothering him. He's told her that his researches might have gotten him into trouble with the CIA. If the detectives show up during the daytime, she tells them that he's on a vacation to Acapulco. She claims that he's been gone for a week and won't be back for another two. **Bullshit Detector** reveals this as transparently deceptive, but she clings to her lie even if the detectives identify themselves as such.

If they first come in the evening, lights will be on in Chip's basement apartment, with its separate entrance, giving Cloris little chance to run interference for her son.

Should the detectives contact him by phone before showing up at his home, Chip agrees to meet them in a few hours, at a neutral location. Then, panicking, he ducks his current service call to go home and scrub his hard drives of all data concerning his conspiracy researches.

If only one or two team members approach Chip's apartment without advance warning, he concludes that the CIA has sent agents to whack him. Chip mounts an attempted escape using his mutant powers. He tries to take his would-be assassins by surprise and web them to the side of his house. If successful, he tries to jump in his deteriorating old compact car and drive off for an undetermined safe location. Chip relents in his escape attempt only when physically stopped, or when convinced that the detectives really are who they claim to be. Given his intense paranoia, it takes a 2-point **Cop Talk** spend to get Chip to accept them as police detectives investigating Sidney Dorris' murder. If Chip remains unconvinced, he'll only answer questions unrelated to his conspiracy theories.

In his late thirties, Chip sports a mop of coarse gray hair. His freckles and piercing blue eyes suggest that he used to be a redhead. Chip dresses sloppily, wearing a plaid short-sleeve dress shirt and mismatched brown corduroy slacks. He smells like breath-enhancing gum.

Detectives must use an ability to get him to talk. **Interrogate** applies if they caught him trying to escape and have him in custody. **Negotiate** also works under this situation; they can offer to forget the resisting arrest charge they could slap him with. **Impersonate** could make them seem like fellow conspiracy buffs. **Flattery**, coupled with an apparent readiness to believe, also does the trick.

Chip runs a website called Conspiracy Forum. Two years ago he was contacted by a man who later revealed himself to be top anamorphological scientist Sidney Dorris. Dorris was responding to a piece he'd written linking the Cube Project, a top-secret CIA operation, with the onset of the SME.

Chip tutored Dorris from the ground up in the murky world of conspiracy theory. Dorris used his resources and legit connections to get information Chip couldn't. Chip wove it all together into a grand tapestry explaining the origins of the SME. Ava Singleton fact checked him—which he found annoying at first, until he realized how much her challenges forced him to solidify his case.

The Cube Project, in a nutshell, was an attempt by the CIA to design a targeted biological weapon that would only kill people with a particular DNA pattern. Theoretically, it could be tuned to be fatal to, say, only members of a particular nuclear family, or every worldwide member of a particular ethnic ancestry. However, a preliminary form of the pathogen escaped into the environment ten years ago, to a quite different effect—triggering the SME.

A couple of weeks ago, he realized that Dorris was going to screw him out of full credit for his work. He was going to announce Chip's SME theory to the world, but didn't even mention him in any of the interviews he gave to hype the announcement.

Sure, he maybe lost his temper a bit and called him Ava on the phone a few times. But that was mild compared to what he could have said! The man tried to steal his entire life.

(core) Dorris didn't even offer a good excuse. Finally he apologized and said he had a lot on his mind, because he was going to be a father for the first time. But then he still didn't promise to mention Chip in his speech. He said it would "confuse matters" and "damage our credibility." He deserved what was coming to him!

But it wasn't Chip who committed the murder. It was the CIA, who wanted to silence him. Duh!

Chip kept warning him to be careful of assassins, but Sidney was dismissive.

(core) He said guns didn't worry him.

Chip is very interested in recovering Sidney's notes, and asks the detectives for help. "It's stolen property, right? That's what cops do. Recover stolen property and return it to its rightful owners."

Chip claims to have been miles away from the hotel at the time of Dorris' death, between service calls. If detectives call the company he works for, they find a three-hour gap between appointments, the second one having been rescheduled by Chip. That leaves more than enough time to have gone to the hotel, killed Dorris, and then performed the second call. A glance at Chip's car reveals a parking lot ticket from the hotel still on his dashboard.

CHIP SILVER

Athletics 4, Driving 2, Filch 4, Fleeing 8, Health 5, Scuffling 2, Shooting 8, Stability 2.

Powers: Webbing 12

HARD HELIX

DR. AARON N. ROSENBLUM

Aaron is, unlike the other witnesses, found through **Research** (see below), as opposed to being mentioned by another possible suspect.

He's an elderly man, his skin papery and near-translucent, his eyes dimming and perpetually watery. Rosenblum dresses nattily in well-kept clothing that looks like it dates from the 1950s. Though his body is failing him, his mental faculties are still fully engaged.

No matter how aggressively the detectives press him, he remains unflaggingly kindly and polite. **Forensic Psychology** reveals that he is deeply shaken by Dorris' death, though too reserved to display his grief to strangers.

When asked why his name appears so often in the dedications to Dorris' books, he explains: "I've known him since he was six years old. We were neighbors when he was a child. He credits me with introducing him to the world of science. For years we've spoken on the phone at least once a week."

Rosenblum is well aware of Dorris' various peccadilloes and improprieties, but is reluctant to discuss them. When he does, it is with the forgiving tone of a doting grandparent: "Like many brilliant men, he was personally troubled."

He supplies the following information in response to appropriately specific questions:

Rosenblum doesn't believe that anyone in Dorris' orbit, or in the anamorphological community, could possibly have killed him. It must have been a robbery attempt gone wrong—perhaps by someone so misguided as to think that Sidney's "invaluable discovery" could be sold for cash.

If Aaron didn't know better, he'd suggest that the detectives make sure the crime wasn't a suicide disguised as a murder. He had a horrible feeling that Sidney's SME theory would turn out to be a humiliating flop—and that Sidney could see it coming.

He had no idea what the theory was, however.

(core) For the past month or so, his calls with Dorris focused on Sidney's growing sense of guilt and depression. He wouldn't explain what he'd done, but said it was at the same time, his deliverance and his damnation, and that he had no idea how to reconcile the two. Rosenblum tried to get him to confide further, but he would only speak in tormented generalities. He tried to get Dorris to seek professional help, but he said it was something he had to work out on his own.

Rosenblum considers Gloria a woman of astonishing patience and forbearance.

Dorris also mistreated Crystal Flores, but she is too good a person to have hurt anyone.

Dorris' career was broken, in his view, by his split from Lucius Quade. If there was lingering animosity, it was from Dorris, toward Quade, not the other way around.

Rosenblum suspected that Dorris was a mutant, but he never confirmed it.

INFORMATION GATHERING

DORRIS' BOOKS

Research turns up all of Dorris' scientific papers and books, including the out-of-print early ones.

Anamorphology, coupled with a quick reading of the books, reveals an early brilliance and technical exactitude which waned sharply over the years. After his departure from the Quade Institute, he publishes only a few papers, none of which would likely have made it into a peer-reviewed journal had his name not been attached to them. Most of his works after that time are books of popular science.

(core) Anyone skimming the books with **Research** (that is, for non-technical information) notes that all but one of the books is dedicated to ANR. In one dedication, he is called "the most loyal of friends." Another says, "To ANR, whose ear is always open." The book which is not dedicated to ANR is *The Soft Helix*, a series of interviews with various anamorphologists—notably not including Lucius Quade. In fact, the only fellow of the Quade Institute profiled is Aaron N. Rosenblum, whose obscure and very technical research focuses on the differences between various mental powers, as measured by changes in brain chemistry. **Anamorphology** pegs him as a much more obscure figure than any of the other scientists profiled in the book.

THE MEDICAL EXAMINATION

The following information can be gleaned by one or more characters performing the examination themselves, using **Forensic Anthropology** and **Ballistics**. Alternately, they can leave the matter in the hands of Mads Jensen and Leonard Northrup. In the latter case, they get a timed result: Northrup calls during a suitable lull in the action to call them over for a computerized demonstration.

Based on the wound trajectory, Dorris' fatal injuries could not have been self-inflicted. They were fired from approximately 1.2 m away, by an assailant firing slightly downwards. Given the location of the wounds on his chest and abdomen, the murderer was most likely Dorris' height, or slightly taller—putting him or her between 5'10" and 6 feet tall.

Of all the suspects, only Crystal Flores and Brian Schmiederer are shorter than this. Galen Birch is too tall to be a likely trigger man.

THE CUBE PROJECT

Research reveals the Cube Project as a frequent subject of conspiracy theorists. It is the Area 51 of a new generation. Various crazy theories link it to everything from cattle mutilations to a secret new Stealth bomber which is invisible to the naked eye. One site lists several dozen accidental deaths and apparently random murders which it links to knowledge of the Cube Project secret. (However, this site thinks that the Cube Project was an effort at mass mind control using electronic devices in weather balloons.) A 2-point **Research** spend debunks the death list as being based on misreported or misinterpreted incidents.

Bureaucracy grants the detective using the ability—and only that detective—a brief, off-the-record meeting with a CIA official named Toler "Tolly" Baldwin, on the understanding that he cannot be called as a witness, or any of what he reveals used as evidence in court. Toler is a bland-looking man in a Brooks Brothers suit who speaks in careful, measured tones. He reveals that the Cube Project was in fact something much more innocuous than the various theories suggest. It was an attempt to produce a super-counterfeit US currency, which could be used untraceably in various operations. This was shut down over nine years ago, on the reasonable objections of the treasury department. When the project threatened to go public, a group of intelligence trainees were tasked, as part of a graduate seminar on disinformation, with covering it up. They did so by generating an all-purpose conspiracy theory. Baldwin seems cagey but the only thing that trips the PC's **Bullshit Detector** comes when he assures, "Of

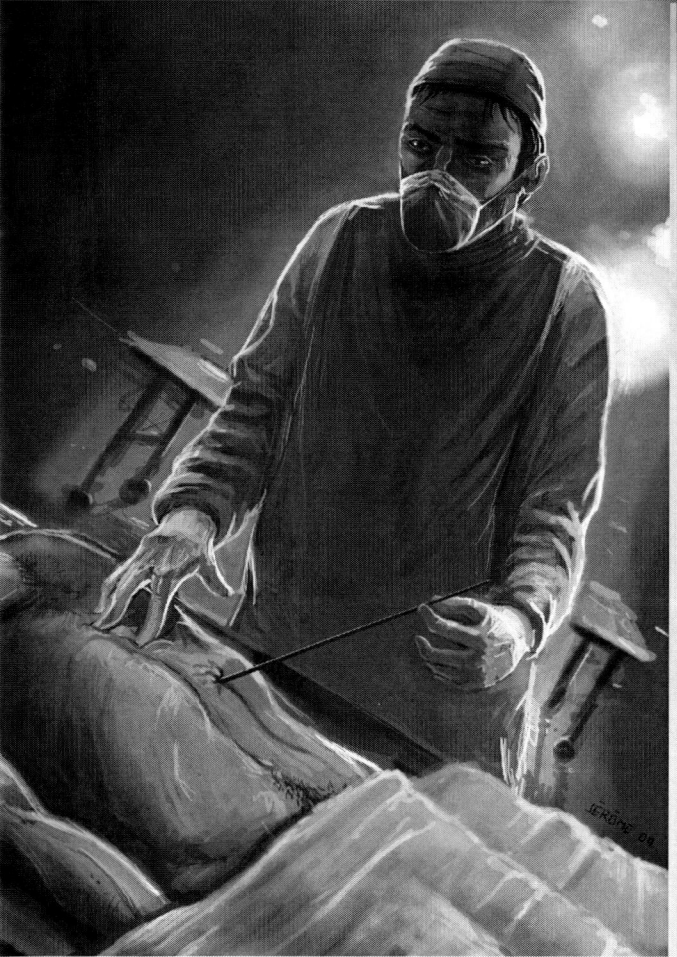

course, we would never dream of doing something like that these days."

AVA'S HOTEL

Sidney was too discreet to be seen showing unprofessional affection for his assistant at a hotel swarming with fellow scientists. He had her stashed in a cheaper establishment. Dorris concluded the day prior to his murder by spending the night with her there.

Unfortunately for Sidney, he long ago lost any board chairmanships that would allow him to conceal financial tracks of his philandering from his wife. She knows this is his favorite hotel when he's visiting the city on his own dime. She drove to the city early and checked in here herself, in hopes of spying on them

The hotel desk clerk is a perky young woman named Paulette Conlon, who gives off a distinct ex-cheerleader vibe. If asked about Sidney and Ava, she says that they had a distressing emotional scene in the lobby at around 6:30 PM. He seemed to be freaking out completely about something, and she was trying, mostly in vain, to calm him down.

She couldn't make out what the discussion was about. Another lady stopped herself from entering the hotel until they finished, then came up to the desk to register. She said, "Can't you tell? She's pregnant."

The woman was Gloria, who made sure that neither Sidney nor Ava spotted her. She registered under a false name—Deena Tynan—but Paulette is able to identify her if shown a photo.

(This scene provides a partially core clue. The detectives can surmise that Gloria somehow learned about Ava's pregnancy, but this bit of legwork confirms it—and places Gloria in town at the time of the murder. If the detectives don't come to this location, look for other ways to introduce Gloria's knowledge of the pregnancy late in the case.)

THE QUADE DIAGRAM

A crucial piece of the puzzle appears on the Quade Diagram. Once they know he had Limb Extension (the core clue from the Galen Birch interview), the players can check out the diagram to see what other powers he's likely to have. Among them is Kinetic Energy Dispersal.

ACTION

DIMWIT INTERLOPERS

With its non-mutant killer, this case offers little inherent opportunity for super-powered action. If your players aren't noticing the lack of it, don't introduce it.

Should you require it, this section provides a red herring action sequence.

A team of full-time stoners and wannabe superhuman secret agents has staked out the hotel, hoping to hijack Dorris' SME secret and sell it to the highest bidder. They are:

BOBBY "NEETCHSTER" NITSZCHE

Athletics 8, Driving 8, Filch 8, Fleeing 4, Health 6, Infiltration 4, Scuffling 8, Shooting 4, Stability 6, Surveillance 4.

Powers: Fire Immunity 6, Fire Projection 12.

Weapon: light firearm 0

VIC "THE BURN" BYRNE

Athletics 9, Driving 7, Filch 9, Fleeing 3, Health 7, Infiltration 3, Scuffling 7, Shooting 5, Stability 5, Surveillance 5.

Powers: High Energy Dispersal 2, Technopathy 6, Telepathy 8.

Weapon: heavy firearm +1

Defect: Attention Deficit Disorder (stage one)

ALICE RAMOS

Athletics 10, Driving 3, Fleeing 7, Health 8, Infiltration 5, Scuffling 8, Shooting 3, Stability 7.

Powers: Command Mammals 4, Environmental Awareness 1, Tracking 4, Olfactory Center 1, Natural Weaponry 12.

Weapon: light firearm 0, natural weaponry +2

Bobby is the group's de facto ringleader. He's a fast-talking dreamer who hopes the money from the sale of Dorris' notes will fund a new rock band he's thinking of forming. As soon as he learns to play an instrument and writes some songs, he's sure he'll be a star.

Vic is your classic lummox, pothead subtype. His ADD makes him hard to interrogate, because he's always losing the thread in any discussion. He wants Bobby to like him and look up to him.

Alice is Bobby's soon to be ex-girlfriend. Her plan is to wait until after they get the money. Bobby and Vic will inevitably indulge in some heavy partying. When they're sleeping it off, she'll split with the dough. She's a tough-looking chick who's clearly invested a lot of time in upper-body development.

That they think a scientific presentation, even if groundbreaking, has significant cash value suggests that these three aren't the sharpest knives in the drawer. When Dorris' notes go missing at the crime scene, they convince themselves that the detectives have them. When given a suitable opportunity, they crash and trash the detectives' vehicle. They try to do it when the team isn't around, but time their assault poorly, so that the PCs are headed back to their car or van as they're tearing it apart.

If captured and interrogated, any of them proves easy to break. They're all eager to roll over on the others. The scene plays as classic interrogation room comedy, featuring lunk-headed, self-justifying criminals.

DRAMA

As an introductory scenario, *The Hard Helix* omits personal storylines. If for some reason you want to run it midway through a series, you might heighten the stakes by drawing on a pre-existing relationship between a detective and one of the iconic supporting characters who appear as suspects, like Galen Birch or Lucius Quade.

WRAP-UP

When they've gathered the available information, the detectives have enough to reconstruct the crime—but no physical evidence. They need to confront the guilty party with what they've figured out, and use it to wring a confession from her.

Here are the prerequisite clues they need to confront Gloria with to her to get her to supply the final leveraged clue that solves the case[1]. She then gives into her guilt and admit what she did:

Gloria knew Ava was pregnant.

This was the last straw; she'd tolerated Sidney's affairs in the past. But this time, he'd not only broken their rule, but he was going to give Ava what he'd denied Gloria—a baby.

Sidney could deflect bullets.

In fact, he deflected one bullet the night he was killed. Gloria's first shot at him took him by surprise, and he deflected the bullet reflexively. But once he realized what was happening, he turned his power off. Depressed and tormented by his conflicting impulses—to seek Gloria's forgiveness, and to have the baby—*he*

let Gloria kill him. This is the point that gets Gloria to break down and confess.

When she confesses, the detectives get their clearance, effectively ending their involvement with the case. They later learn that she entered a plea bargain agreement, getting the sentence at the low end of the scale for premeditated murder.

---

[1] Prerequisite and leveraged clues are described on *Mutant City Blues* p. 157

HARD HELIX

⚛ CHARACTER QUICK REFERENCE

Toler "Tolly" Baldwin - CIA official

Lucy Bellaver - Police photographer

Galen Birch - Billionaire mutant

Vernetta Brown - lecturer in anamorphology from Regent University in Virginia

Vic "the Burn" Byrne - stoner wannabe superhero

Paulette Conlon – hotel desk clerk

Gloria Dorris – Sidney Dorris' wife

Sidney Dorris - Controversial scholar of anamorphology

Harry Fields - Hotel manager

Crystal Flores - Former research assistant of Dorris, currently adjunct professor of anamorphology at the University Of Texas A&M

Milton Gaines - freelance writer

Isabel Gameros - housecleaning staffer

Dr. Mala Gowariker - heads the anamorphology department of the University of Delhi, India

Mads Jensen - Medical examiner

Bobby "Neetchster" Nitszche - stoner wannabe superhero

Conrad Priestley - Anti-mutant activist

Magda Priestley – Conrad Priestley's mother

Lucius Quade - father of anamorphology

Alice Ramos - stoner wannabe superhero

Ed "the Ted" Riley – Criminalist

Dr. Aaron N. Rosenblum - childhood friend of Sidney Dorris

Brian Schmiederer - City councilor

Chip Silver - Certified paranoid

Cloris Silver – Chip Silver's mother

Ava Singleton – Dorris' mistress

Deena Tynan – alias of Gloria Dorris

THE VANISHERS

The squad's intervention in a jewelry store robbery leads them into an operation against a mutant-bolstered mob.

BACKSTORY

The gambling debts of flamboyant jewelry store manager "Broadway" Bob Border leave him no choice but to acquiesce to the demands of mob boss Jason "the Machine" Vetroni.

THE CRIME

Border calls the HCIU during a robbery in progress. Mutant punks are emptying his vault!

THE INVESTIGATION

After the prelude, **A Frantic Call,** squad members may be able to apprehend the apparent robbers during the initial action sequence scene, **Four Punks and a Patsy**. Oddly, most of the contents of Border's vault remain missing even when the perps are captured. Have the gold and jewels really vanished into thin air, via an unknown mutant power, as Border claims? Meanwhile, the none-too-bright heisters confess to being controlled by a **Criminal Mastermind** they only know as a disembodied voice on the other end of a phone line.

THE TWIST

If the detectives instead heed their instincts about **Broadway Bob**, they may come to suspect that the disappearance of his inventory occurred by more mundane means.

THE CULPRITS

Bob's Bookmaker cagily admits to having sold the jeweler's debt to the mob.

When they get another distress call from Bob, detectives may be tempted to let him stew in his own juices—even though he claims to be driving a **Coffin On Wheels**. The dynamite used in his car bomb leads them to look into a **Hijacking Ring**. This puts them in touch with FBI agents working **A Long-term Case** against the Vetroni crime family. This up-and-coming mob group illustrates the mutation event's impact on the old-line Mafia. Can the HCIU step into the breach, putting together the takedown that has long eluded the feds?

SCENES

A FRANTIC CALL

SCENE TYPE: OPENER

It's a slow week at the Heightened Crimes Investigation Unit. The squad hasn't caught a new case of any note for eight days.

Start by having each of the players detail what they do when they're in the office and have no work of any urgency on their plates. Where possible, introduce minor comic complications to their various efforts to look busy.

Then a call comes in, patched through by dispatch. It's a recording of a hushed 911 call placed moments ago. The voice is that of a middle-aged man with a peculiarly unplaceable accent that wanders halfway between English and Australian:

CALLER: Please you've got to help me quickly. This is Broadway Bob Border, of Broadway Jewelry, [insert street address here] and I am being robbed, right now, in my store, by mutants.

EMERGENCY OPERATOR: Mr. Border, what can you tell me about the—

HARD HELIX

CALLER: Can't risk any more—just get here, now! Please!

(If you can't do an odd half-English, half-Aussie accent, substitute another mixed accent you can sustain.)

FOUR PUNKS AND A PATSY
SCENE TYPE: ACTION

Cut quickly from the call to the squad's arrival on the scene.

If the players seem invested in the question of how to get there quickly, and come up with an entertaining and super-heroically plausible way of using one or more powers to get there fast, they gain an advantage: robbers Horace Monette and Gabe Losey have failed to properly insert their clips into their pistols. Their first attempts to fire their guns automatically fail, costing each of them 2 Shooting points. This advantage pertains only if the squad takes action immediately upon arrival. If they pause to plan or do something else, Soto and Losey then put their guns in good order.

If the squad members arrive with merely ordinary dispatch, Soto and Losey have already spotted the problems with their guns and successfully reinserted the clips.

In the event that the players do gain the advantage for extra speed, make sure that they learn, presumably during the later interrogation sequence, that they got an advantage by arriving on the scene quickly.

Upon arrival, four armed robbers are in the midst of robbing Broadway Bob: Gabe Losey, Horace Monette, Cristina McGonagle, and Alex Soto. A fifth accomplice, Sarah Soto, circles the block in a banged-up van, waiting to serve as getaway driver. Along with Bob Border, there are two employees and one customer in the store. Sales clerks Georgiana Koenig and Amy Ore have been bound and gagged behind the store counter. Gabe has his weapon trained on them. The customer, former linebacker Larry Evans, sits immobile with his back against a display case, his knees tucked under his chin. Horace has just zapped him with emotion control, plunging him into a paralyzing depression. Horace's gun is pointed at Larry, just in case he snaps out of it.

Cristina is inside Bob's closet-sized walk-in vault, ripping open lock boxes and pouring their contents into a series of duffel bags. Alex stands immediately outside

 YOUR CASH FOR MY GOLD!

Unless characters specify that they don't watch television, they're familiar with the commercials for Broadway Jewelry. These air incessantly in time slots with cheap ad rates. Cheaply produced, they feature the shop's owner, a paunchy, balding man festooned with gold rings, shouting energetically into the camera.

Get up and demonstrate, reading the above script (transfer to an index card if necessary) while wildly gesticulating:

"This is Broadway Bob Border of Broadway Jewelry and I'm here to tell you that swapping gold for cash has never been easier! You have gold! I have cash! Come on down with your gold and I will physically slam cash into your hand! Physically slam! Is that why they call me the Cash Slammer? Think about it! Why else would they call me that? Get slammed with cash — at Broadway Bob Border's Broadway Jewelry, [insert street address here]! Do it todaaayyyy!!!"

the vault door, his clawed hands wrapped around the throat of a kneeling Broadway Bob. Near Bob's knee are the remnants of his crushed cell phone.

As is common in pawn and jewelry shops, customers must be buzzed in through a locked door, before which they are required to stand in a claustrophobic foyer under the scrutiny of a video camera. This entire structure has been torn away from the front of the store. It is now a twisted sculpture of bent aluminum and broken glass. (Cristina ripped it apart with her Strength power.)

The robbers are habitual but not hardened criminals. If they can turn an arrest attempt into a hostage situation, they will, attempting to bargain the lives of the customers for their freedom. Otherwise, they try to shoot their way out. Their goal is to escape, not to kill cops, but if they have to use lethal force to escape, they're panicked enough to do it. As soon as two of them are incapacitated or taken into custody, the others drop their guns and surrender. An exception is the overmuscled Cristina; once enraged, she doesn't back down. After having observed her in red-faced, screaming action for a round, a detective with **Forensic Psychology** concludes that she's the most aggressive member of the bunch, though not its unofficial leader. (That would be Alex.) In other words, it's a good idea to try to take her out early on.

Also during the second round:

- the character with **Streetwise** best positioned to look out the store window, seeing Sarah Soto's van drive by for the second time, realizes that it's the getaway vehicle.
- **Forensic Pathology** indicates that Gabe, Alex and Horace are all crackheads. Sarah, when seen close up, also shows the telltale scabs, sallow skin, and signs of premature aging typical of hardcore rock cocaine abuse.

Sarah and Gabe are both norms; the other robbers are all mutants.

GABE LOSEY

Identifying features: 5'11", 130 lbs, Caucasian, close-cropped dark hair, scratched up, gold framed glasses with tape on nose piece.

Athletics 2, Fleeing 8, Health 2, Scuffling 2, Shooting 6

Weapon: .22 pistol 0

HORACE MONETTE

Identifying features: 5' 8", 142 lbs, Caucasian, dreadlocks, soul patch, multiple tattoos, including large *fleur du lys* on neck.

Athletics 2, Fleeing 8, Health 2, Scuffling 2, Shooting 6

Powers: Emotion Control 7 (rating 19)

Weapon: .22 pistol 0

CRISTINA MCGONAGLE

Identifying features: 5' 8", 180 lbs, Caucasian, heavily muscled, severely cut blond hair, acute acne, teeth surgically implanted to resemble mutant fangs

Athletics 12, Health 12, Scuffling 8, Shooting 4

Powers: Gills 4, Regeneration 8, Strength 15 (rating 25), Toxin Immunity (Inhaled) 4

Weapon: unarmed +4, or +1 for every 4 points in Strength pool, whichever is lower; .45 pistol +1

ALEX SOTO

Identifying features: 5' 6", 120 lbs, Hispanic, shaved head, blue eyes.

Athletics 6, Fleeing 8, Health 8, Scuffling 6, Shooting 4

HARD HELIX

Powers: High Energy Dispersal 8, Limb Extension 4, Kinetic Energy Dispersal 8, Natural Weaponry 6.

Weapon: claws +2, .45 pistol +1

SARAH SOTO

Identifying features: 5'4", 135 lbs, Caucasian, brunette, brown eyes, heavy scar tissue on left earlobe (remnant of bite injury)

Athletics 2, Driving 8, Health 2, Scuffling 2, Shooting 6

Weapon: .22 pistol 0

CRIMINAL MASTERMIND
SCENE TYPE: RED HERRING

Once apprehended and separated, the jewelry store robbers roll on one another after only token efforts on the part of their interrogators.

Gabe, a jumpy, profusely sweating addict, promises to tell all he knows in exchange for the promise of a reduced sentence and the opportunity to go out and score one last time. (**Negotiation**.)

Horace will easily believe, not without foundation, that the others will roll on him if he doesn't do it to them first. (**Interrogation**.)

Cristina makes self-incriminating admissions if goaded into losing her temper. (**Interrogation**.)

Sarah, a self-sacrificing and protective wife, talks if promised lenient treatment not for herself, but for Alex. (**Negotiation**.)

Alex starts out trying to make anyone else, including his wife, out to be the ringleader, but crumples when detectives disbelieve him. (**Bullshit Detector**.)

No one but Alex knows very much about the motivation behind the heist. He, Gabe and Horace have been non-violent break-and-enter specialists for nearly two years. Cristina recently barged into the derelict rowhouse they've been using as a squat and declared herself their new roommate. The others suspect (correctly) that she's responsible for a series of muggings in the area.

TERRIFIED WITNESSES

Bob's employees and customer have little useful information for detectives. All of them are clearly traumatized by the robbery. Use dialogue with them to emphasize the reckless human impact of the robbery scam.

Larry Evans can barely summon the motivation to answer police questions. He wonders aloud if live is worth living in a crazy world where crooks can just rip open the storefronts of places they want to rob. **Influence Detection** shows that he has been hit with a mind control power. On a 1-point **Forensic Psychology** spend, he agrees to seek professional help for his induced mental state, and realizes that Horace gave him a weird, penetrating look just before he went into shutdown mode.

Matronly sales clerk Georgiana Koenig says she heard the bald one (Alex) and the big butch one (Cristina) exchange angry, whispered words about who was in charge. The bald one said that "the voice" wouldn't take it well if she screwed up the operation.

All the wispy young sales clerk Amy Ore can say is that her mother is going to kill her once she finds out the store was robbed. Her mother was worried that the jewelry store was a dangerous place to work, on account of stick-up artists and the like. Amy begs the detectives not to drag her into court. All she can remember is being scared out of her mind.

Regarding the robbery, the others know only that Alex came up with the idea about a month ago, and that he got the guns from an unknown source, specifically for this score. Aside from Sarah, they all assume that he got the idea from watching Broadway Bob's memorably annoying TV commercials. (Thanks to Horace, they have stolen power and a small TV in their squat.)

Sarah knows that Alex got a cell phone from his dealer, streetnamed Grassy, just before he announced the robbery plan, and that he's been going off to talk on it ever since.

Alex, if induced to talk, says that he was contacted by a "criminal mastermind" who promised him and his crew lucrative careers as his followers. They would get to jet around the world, performing dangerous missions. They could stay in the best hotels, eat awesome food, and party like there's no tomorrow. The jewelry heist was an audition, to show what they could do. The mastermind chose the target and told him when to hit it. To consider the mission a success, they had to get the vault open and empty its contents without serious injury to anyone inside the store. If they failed in this, they would be hunted down and destroyed. "That's the exact phrase he used. Hunted down and destroyed." They would be allowed to keep anything they took; the mastermind was interested in what they could do, not a cut of the take. He supplied the guns, which were dropped at the squat doorstep in the dead of night by unseen operatives. The mastermind never identified himself, not even with a code or street name. His voice was electronically altered, like in the movies.

(The bit about being hunted down and destroyed is an empty threat. The "mastermind", Vetroni, takes no further interest in Alex or his buddies after they're incarcerated. Player efforts to protect the robbers or use them as bait to attract the mastermind might serve as an entertaining if fruitless plot tangent.)

A trawl of Alex's scummy neighborhood with **Streetwise** turns up a number of Grassy's erstwhile clients, but no Grassy. He hasn't been seen in weeks. One dealer, Sean "Twan" Bridewell, 21, says that Grassy ceded him his turf after leaving to pursue a "business opportunity" in Vegas. (It sounds like the Vetronis had Grassy whacked, but they really did send him out of town. However, when he gets there, he'll find that the potential of the new opportunity has been greatly exaggerated.)

BROADWAY BOB

SCENE TYPE: CORE

Given the odd notes in the "criminal mastermind" story, the squad may become suspicious of Broadway Bob on their own. If not, they get a phone call on the next business day from Ray Ashe, a claims adjuster from Pacific Partners Insurance. Bob Border has filed a compensation claim for half a million dollars worth of missing merchandise and needs to confirm the losses with the primary detective on the case.

In the unlikely event that one or more of the robbers escaped during the opening sequence, it may seem possible that some of the gold and jewels are still missing. In most outcomes of that scene, the detectives will be surprised to hear of the claim. Anything in the gang's duffel bags has been tagged as evidence. What's up with the supposed additional losses?

When interviewed, Border says that a check of the vault after the robbery showed that nearly $495,000 worth of merchandise (wholesale value) was missing. He attributes this to a mutant power used either by the robbers or perhaps an unknown confederate. **Anamorphology** confirms what the players probably already know: no documented mutant power works that way. Bob waves away any such objections; he's no an expert in anamorphology. All he knows is that half a million bucks worth of his gold and diamonds disappeared during a robbery—and he wants the detectives to do something about it. In the meantime, he expects them to sign off on his insurance claim. A player asking to evaluate his honesty with **Bullshit Detector** concludes that Bob is an experienced and confident BS artist. He may very well be drawing on that skill now, but who knows?

Bob provides a list of the missing merchandise. **Forensic Accounting** notes that all of the listed pieces are ordinary, interchangeable pieces: gold coins and bars, or very basic rings with gems. The $27,000 worth of pieces Soto's gang had on them when arrested were the most expensive in Border's inventory—but also the hardest to fence.

(core a) **Law** tells the detectives that their suspicions of Bob aren't enough to get a search warrant for his financials. But what he may not realize is that the fine print on his policy with Pacific Partners allows them full access to all of his personal or private accounts—and the right to pass any untoward details they find along to law enforcement.

Asked to dive into Border's bank records, the phlegmatic, deadpan Ray Ashe is only too happy to oblige.

A few days later (the time jump can be elided over if the squad has no other leads they'd like to follow), Ashe shows up at the HCIU offices to share the results of his search. **Forensic Accounting** confirms what Ashe has found: multiple unexplained withdrawals from Border's personal and business accounts over a period of several years. The amounts escalate steadily over time, with recent withdrawals hitting the $50,000 mark.

HARD HELIX

The players may suspect that these are gambling debts; Ray Ashe certainly does. **Trivia** shows that the escalations coincide with major sporting events, including March Madness and the Super Bowl.

Grilled about this, Bob unconvincingly asserts that his withdrawals were made to help a friend with unexpected medical expenses. He has no receipts and declines to supply a name for this friend. If pressed further, or threatened with an insurance fraud charge, he lawyers up. (His lawyer is Vivien Coleman, a stone-faced woman in a slightly outdated power suit.)

(core b) **Law** suggests that the red flags in his bank records, coupled with the fishy insurance claim, will net them a search warrant for Bob's phone records.

(core c) Bob's cell phone shows numerous calls to a single phone number, coincident with the payouts from his accounts. The cell belongs to John "Heck" Reid; **Streetwise** identifies him as a longtime bookie.

Research shows that Reid's rap sheet is surprisingly clean for a career bookmaker. It contains numerous letters noting favors provided to the police over the years. Never formally designated as a confidential informant, he's been strategically slipping crucial tips to the department since 1968. No doubt these account for his light arrest record. **Cop Talk** suggests that they should think twice before burning this veteran asset to the force.

BOB'S BOOKMAKER
SCENE TYPE: CORE

A call to Heck Reid's cell results in a resigned agreement to meet with squad members—though not in public, and nowhere near a police station. He brings his characteristic hangdog expression to a mutually agreed discreet location. Heck pops antacids pills throughout the conversation. He readily admits to taking increasingly heavy sports bets from Broadway Bob over a period of six to seven years.

(core) If offered yet another recommendation letter for his police jacket (**Negotiation**), he's willing to tell them "enough to get you started, but not enough to get me whacked." Assuming the detectives agree to this, he says he sold Border's debt to a third party—who shall remain nameless.

Streetwise (or basic logic) dictates that Reid operates with the blessing of—that is, pays protection to—an organized crime figure. Reid blanches when asked to name the mobster who collects his dues. "Remember what I said earlier about not getting myself whacked?"

(If word filters back to Vetroni that Heck told detectives even this much, he will be found murdered by gunshot. The untraceable weapon will be found at the otherwise clean crime scene.)

COFFIN ON WHEELS
SCENE TYPE: CORE

Speaking of getting whacked, Broadway Bob's mobbed up co-conspirators have decided that he's likely to crack under the strain and confess to insurance fraud. They decide to dispose of him with a fancy car bomb.

A call from Border, patched through dispatch to the primary detective's cell phone, draws the squad into the scene. Unless interrupted, calmed down (**Reassurance**), and carefully guided to explain the situation step-by-step, Bob's communication consists solely of hysterical pleas to come to his aid immediately.

Here's what they get out of him after calming him down:

- He's currently in his Rolls Royce, on a major highway, about a three minute drive from the squad's current location.

- He keeps a travel humidor next to the driver's seat. A minute ago, he reached into it for a cigar and found that it had been tampered with.

- Instead of cigars, it contained a block of electronic components and a digital timer. When he opened the humidor, the timer started counting down.

- Bob now sees tiny wires running out of the case into the back seat. Craning his neck, he can see what look like sticks of dynamite taped under the passenger seat.

- The mechanism in the box includes a mercury bubble thingy. (**Explosive Devices** indicates that this is an anti-tamper mechanism, meant to set the bomb off instantaneously if anyone attempts to defuse it. Now that the bomb has primed, the anti-tamper device may well trigger it if Bob hits the brakes, or the vehicle is suddenly jolted in any way.)

When Bob calls them, he has 5:38 left on the timer. Of course, this will continue to tick down as the characters speak to him, so if they're smart they'll head his way as soon as they realize what's going on, continuing the cell conversation as they travel to him.

Whether they save Bob is a matter of player creativity and applied super powers. Assign Difficulties of 4 or so to reasonably credible actions undertaken in a rescue attempt. A non-exclusive list of possible solutions includes:

- Allowing the dynamite to detonate, then using Suppress Explosion to snuff out the blast

- Driving alongside and using Disintegration or Transmutation to destroy the mechanism

- Driving alongside and using Reduce Temperature to freeze its mechanism

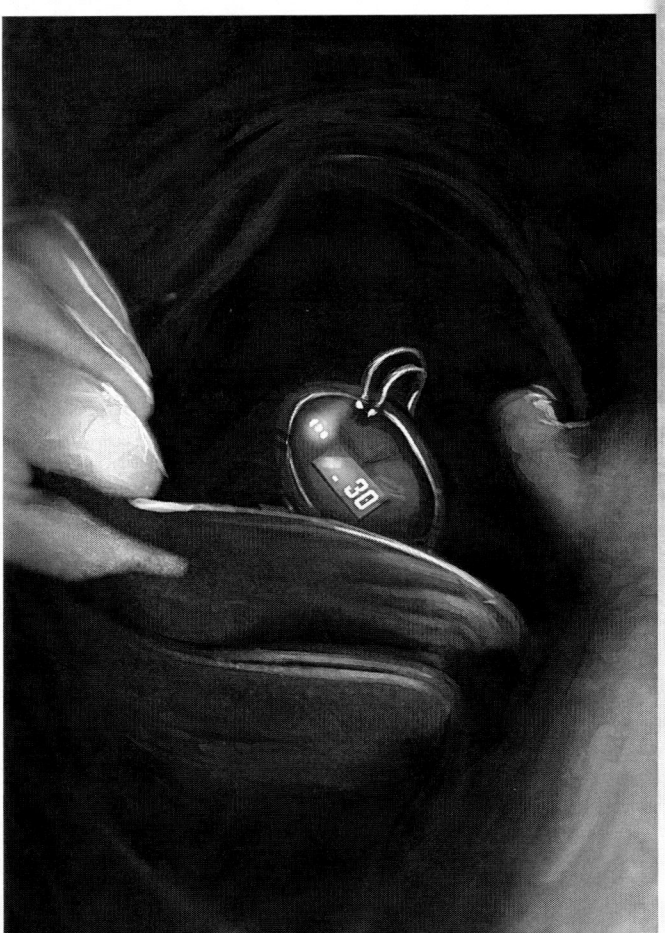

- Placing a Shield around Bob to protect him from the explosion

- Teleporting into the car and using Mechanics (Difficulty 4; character must have Explosive Devices) to defuse the bomb.

- Using Technokinesis to make the bomb shut itself down

Bob has a Health pool of 4. The bomb is a class 3 explosive (see *Mutant City Blues* p. 99) but behaves differently while contained within the vehicle. Anyone inside the car when it blows suffers three instances of +2 damage. The blast has only a 4m debris radius.

If detonated outside the car, it operates according to the normal rules for an explosive of its class.

It is conceivable that Bob could be inside the car when it blows but still survive or even be brought back from death by the Healing power.

If the bomb goes off, the totaled vehicle and the surrounding roadway become a crime scene. Otherwise, the parked car becomes the scene.

The means by which the core clue is gathered varies depending on whether the bomb goes off or can be examined in its unexploded state.

First off, **Explosive Devices** suggests that this bomb was made by a someone of impressive technical sophistication working in an unconventional way. The most efficient way to kill a guy with a car bomb is to wire it through the ignition, so it blows when the engine is turned on. Standard car bomber practice is also to fix the bomb to the underside of the chassis. This was both more work than the usual car bomb, and imposed a higher chance of failure.

Forensic Psychology points out that the bomb's design suggests a sense of malice: Border was supposed to spot the bomb, and spend a prolonged last few moments anticipating his awful demise. Its placement in Bob's portable humidor suggests a close awareness of his idiosyncratic personal habits. The gesture might be interpreted as a jab at his inflated ego or lifestyle pretensions.

(core a and c; if exploded) **Chemistry** finds tiny plastic taggant chips in the blast residue. **Explosive Devices** shows that these identifying components are not

HARD HELIX

required in dynamite made for the domestic market. Only a few jurisdictions, including Switzerland, require their use. **Research** shows that a shipment of dynamite headed for shipment to Switzerland was hijacked six months ago. The case officer on this still-active file is Special Agent Lin Mosswood of the Bureau of Alcohol, Tobacco, and Firearms.

(core a through c; not exploded) **Explosive Devices** finds that the dynamite is factory made but that the identifying information on the stick casings has been scraped away. **Document Analysis** recovers enough traces of the factory marks and serial numbers to trace the dynamite to a manufacturer named Regalis, located in an adjoining state. **Research** shows that a shipment from this factory was hijacked six months ago. That the case officer on this still-active file is Special Agent Lin Mosswood of the Bureau of Alcohol, Tobacco, and Firearms.

The attempt on his life does not render Bob more forthcoming—assuming he survives at all. He loudly refuses to cooperate, as if expecting mob moles within the police department to overhear and report his silence back to Vetroni.

Vetroni probably gives up on having Bob killed at this point. However, if you need an antagonist reaction during the later takedown sequence and can logically justify his ordering another shot at Bob, you can always insert a second assassination attempt.

HIJACKING RING
SCENE TYPE: CORE

Special Agent Lin (short for "Lincoln") Mosswood meets squad members in his cubicle in the local ATF field office. He wears snakeskin cowboy boots under the standard-issue medium-priced dark suit that is de rigeur for federal agents. Mosswood is a meaty, barrel-chested man in his late fifties capable of swaggering while seated. He speaks with a slight southwestern twang. When the squad appears, he tests them by asking about their jobs as mutant cops. He resists divulging information about the case until they show, using **Cop Talk**, that they're bona fide law enforcement, and not a gaggle of affirmative action goofballs. His queries take a needling tone that borders on anti-mutant bigotry.

Even when they prove themselves worthy of old-school respect, Mosswood refuses to turn over his files. **Bureaucracy** recognizes this as standard federal agent turf protection-slash-obstructionism, the kind that local cops just have to swallow.

Mosswood reveals the following, in response to specific questions:

- The hijacking took place at night on a two-lane highway not far from your mutant city.

- The driver, Dolph Delaughter of Pine Lake, Georgia, was unharmed by the robbers, who wore gloves and ski masks and spoke very little.

- This was Delaughter's third hijacking in his long career as a long haul trucker; he described these guys as the "most professional" of the three.

- In cases like these, the drivers or somebody in shipping is in on it, but Mosswood took Delaughter for a straight shooter.

- The stretch of highway where Delaughter's truck was ambushed is a frequent target for hijacks.

- None of the other hijacks were of explosives or guns, but others were of booze and cigarettes, which also fall under Mosswood's purview.

- There have also been thefts of truck contents including power tools, electronic equipment, swimming pool kits, air conditioners, and freeze-dried steaks.

- (core) On these latter cases, Mosswood has been coordinating with Special Agent Shane Lerner, team leader of an anti-organized crime task force at the FBI.

Dolph Delaughter is on the road, but can be reached by cell phone. A genial older gentleman, he confirms the details he gave to Mosswood.

A LONG-TERM CASE
SCENE TYPE: CORE

Unlike Lin Mosswood, the youthful, ambitious FBI agent Shane Lerner is happy to receive input and assistance from a squad of mutant cops. He's had the munitions hijacking on his gigantic cork board of interconnected crimes for months now, and has reached a chokepoint in his investigation. He knows who he's after, but just can't shake loose enough evidence to start making arrests.

He's building a case against city mob figure Jason "the Machine" Vetroni. Vetroni has come from nowhere to seize control of the Fiorillo crime family in a few short years.

Lerner provides the following As to the player's Qs:

- Until Vetroni took it over, the Fiorillo outfit was an old-school Mafia outfit, on the way out. Made guys had turned informer. Asian, Caribbean and Russian gangs were encroaching on their key businesses. Mob leaders were headed to jail.

- Vetroni, who came up as a street soldier in the outfit, muscled out the remaining old crew and revitalized the organization.

- His secret: mutant powers.

- Before "the Machine", classic mob guys reacted with their usual insularity to mutants, even within their own ranks. Weird powers kept you from rising in the organization.

- Word is that Vetroni kept his own genetic status a secret while reaching out to other disenfranchised mutant mobsters from across the country. He recruited them as allies, then used their powers to push out the old Fiorillo group.

- Now all of the new mob's captains are young mutants like Vetroni. (Lerner is misinformed here; there are still a couple of DNA-standard holdovers.)

- Lerner and his small team of agents have some intelligence on his operation, but nothing they can take to court. Most of it is second-hand scuttlebutt from low-level informants.

- They have secured a wire tap for Vetroni's home, and for his apparent HQ in a suburban sandwich joint. However, for some unknown reason, the wiretap devices always fail. "The Machine" is frustratingly careful in his phone use.

- Vetroni's super powers are thought to be of the mental variety.

- The route where the dynamite was heisted has been a hunting preserve for Fiorillo family hijackers for generations.

- Heck Reid's connections to the Fiorillos go way back; he undoubtedly pays protection to Vetroni through one of his captains. Vetroni could easily be the guy who bought Broadway Bob's gambling debts.

The remainder of this scenario is player-driven, as they liaise with the feds in an attempt to crack open the Vetroni organization. Profiles of the Vetroni crew are presented in sourcebook style, followed by a list of possible player approaches you can prepare for.

THE VETRONI OUTFIT

This section outlines the personalities, interrelationships and activities of the mob the squad must take down in order to close the books on the Broadway Bob case. The jewel store insurance scam pans out as a comparatively minor element in a much larger criminal conspiracy.

Any of the mobsters detailed in this section can be armed with any type of gun, if in a situation where they think they'll need them. They all have firearms concealed in their vehicles. However, they don't pack heat casually. They don't want to be hit with weapons charges if searched by the cops.

A sub-head lists each mobster's main criminal activity. Most dabble in other kinds of action on the side, and anyone can be called upon at any moment to engage in violence on behalf of the crew, up to and including murder.

Information in the profiles that would reasonably have been gathered during the prior FBI surveillance operation can also be provided by Shane Lerner. This can also be gathered by polling detectives' underworld contacts with **Streetwise**. Hints that might lead the squad to the mobsters' various dark secrets might be available on 2- or 3-point spends. Spends never provide the entire secret, just a path toward it.

HARD HELIX

JASON "THE MACHINE" VETRONI
BOSS

Jason Vetroni is third generation Mafia. His grandfather ran a numbers operation and fenced stolen appliances for the Fiorillo family. His father and two uncles were all street soldiers for the outfit. All three met premature and somewhat ignominious ends. His dad, a mean drunk, quarreled with a superior and was found in the trunk of an abandoned car. His oldest uncle was knifed to death while collecting a debt. The younger one died in a car accident while fleeing police with a car full of laundered cash.

The shame of the older generation's failures hung over Jason, forcing him to work aggressively to make his bones. When he discovered his mutant powers, he concealed them from his mob elders. Branching out into murder for hire, he specialized in vehicular homicides that looked like accidents. Eventually, old man Fiorillo realized that he had to be using a mutant power to take control of the victims' vehicles. Even though he was twice the asset to the family that his father or uncles had been, Jason found himself repeatedly passed over for promotion. So he used another of his mutant powers, one granting him the ability to see the best possible way forward among any set of choices. His mutant cognition laid out a plan to recruit similarly sidelined mutant mobsters from across the continent.

Vetroni still faced limits on the sorts of guys he could bring into his crew, without triggering the alarm bells of his then-superiors. Somebody in some branch of the Mafia somewhere had to vouch for each new hire. When Jason had enough guys on his side, he started bumping off the already hard-pressed old-timers. Eventually the remnants of the family caved and made him boss.

Extremely young for a mob leader, the 31-year-old Vetroni has abandoned the thuggish track suit attire of his salad days in favor of restrained business attire. He owes the tight muscles draped tautly over his lanky frame to his time spent behind the punching bag at a boxing club he covertly owns. With outsiders, he adopts a smooth, charming demeanor. He maintains the pose of a new corporate breed of mobster even with his confederates, peppering his statements with only slightly misused business jargon. Whacking a guy in his family is "downsizing." Subordinates expected to run several criminal operations at once are "multi-tasking." No-show jobs[1] are called "virtual outsourcing."

Aware that every mob leader needs to seem like a good Catholic family man, Jason married pretty former cheerleader Anna Carboni shortly after ascending to his leadership post. She is now pregnant with what will be their first child. Breaking with mob tradition, Jason so far keeps no permanent mistress on the side, though of course he fools around with party girls and strippers now that the wife is knocked up.

Vetroni rarely engages in direct criminal activity now that he's in charge. Instead he assigns illegal businesses to his captains, who pay him a percentage of their earnings. He invests the money mostly in property, knowing enough about business not to trust those crooks on Wall Street. His portfolio of legit businesses includes a small dry-cleaning chain, a car wash, and three slum apartment buildings, in addition to the sandwich shop and boxing club. None of these

---

1 In this classic scam, owners of businesses under mob influence are forced to put his guys on the payroll and grant them benefits, even though they do no work.

are in his own name; they're run for him by otherwise legitimate citizens.

In a break from his usual hands-off management style, Jason personally planned and executed the Broadway Jewelry scam. His altered voice—created by using Technokinesis to manipulate his cell phone's audio chip—is that of Soto's so-called "criminal mastermind." During his limited interactions with the obstreperous Broadway Bob, Jason conceived an intense hatred of the man. This is why he wanted Border to see the car bomb, and know that he was going to die—for the crime of annoying Jason "the Machine" Vetroni.

JASON "THE MACHINE" VETRONI

Athletics 8, Driving 4, Health 12, Scuffling 8, Shooting 4

Powers: Cognition*[2], Lightning Decisions 4, Technokinesis 12, Technopathy 2, Precision Memory *

PAUL "THE LAWYER" MARTELLI

LOAN SHARKING

A good fifteen years older than any of Vetroni's other recruits, Paul Martelli came to his attention through a jail house contact who claimed that his connected cell mate could project his thoughts. Upon his release from a Philadelphia[3]-area prison on extortion and assault charges, Vetroni brought Martelli into his crew. White-haired and heavily scarred from his prison stay, Martelli is a devoted old schooler who just happened to be unlucky enough to "catch the mutation." He favors outlandish suits and jewelry straight out of *Goodfellas*. While in jail he became a self-taught legal practitioner, burying the system in groundless motions. He learned enough to advise Jason on legal issues. His defense of the family extends to the mutant realm: he regularly scans Vetroni's crew for signs of mental influence. Martelli quickly discovers any mental powers used by the PCs on members of the outfit.

---

[2] Powers marked with an asterisk appear in the *Mutant City Blues* rules assuming their use by PCs. For supporting characters, simply portray them as if they possess superior decision-making abilities, heightened memory, and so on.

[3] Vetroni's cronies are meant to come from all around the continent. If one of the cities mentioned in a profile is your mutant city, change the reference to another city.

His once-beautiful wife Violetta can be crass and demanding, to which Martelli reacts with sullen forbearance. He appears at social events with the still-beautiful Other Violetta, a mistress who confusingly bears the same name as his wife. Martelli's children are Paul Junior, 19, and Chrissy, 17, both of whom are in denial about their dad's line of work and headed for college and straight jobs.

Martelli hates cops and is too close-mouthed to say anything to them that falls outside the category of verbal abuse.

Vetroni assigned him the job of storing and eventually fencing the jewels that were pre-stolen from Broadway Bob's store. Martelli placed them under the floorboards of a barn on a disused farm owned under his wife's name in a rural area near the city. If the detectives conduct a search for properties under the names of his family members, **Research** turns up the location of the farm. Martelli is nervous about the jewels and travels there every few weeks to check up on them. A successful around-the-clock Surveillance (Difficulty 5; Martelli is a cagey customer) eventually tracks him to the site.

PAUL "THE LAWYER" MARTELLI

Athletics 4, Driving 4, Health 8, Scuffling 12, Shooting 2

Powers: Detect Influence 10, Suppress Influence 20, Telepathy 8

DANNY "FLIPPER" DE FILIPPO

BOOKMAKING

When his buddies in the Chicago mob discovered that Danny De Filippo could navigate by sonar, they did what any self-respecting made men would do—they chained him inside a derelict van and drove it over a pier. Fortunately for Danny, he also had a set of gills. Having heard that a guy in mutant city was recruiting experienced wise guys with powers, he made his way to Vetroni's doorstep. After a probationary period to prove his trustworthiness to Paulie the Lawyer, Danny won acceptance by upping the earnings of the gang's bookmaking operation. Danny is the link between Heck Reid and Vetroni, and helped arrange the purchasing of Broadway Bob's debt.

HARD HELIX

Danny's cheerful attitude and love of the free-spending lifestyle mask his dangerous side. He exhibits an almost puppyish loyalty toward Jason, who he regards as a savior. Danny takes seething umbrage at any slight directed toward the boss.w

A stocky young guy with blocky features, Danny has been seeing Martelli's 17-year-old daughter Chrissy behind his back. Although Danny has no intention of flipping on his colleagues, knowledge of this very unwise relationship could be used as leverage over him (**Negotiation**.)

DANNY "FLIPPER" DE FILIPPO

Athletics 6, Driving 6, Health 6, Scuffling 4, Shooting 6

Powers: Gills 8, Sonar 12, Sonic Blast 12

AL "POPPER" SOLDATI
HIJACKING / CORRUPT CONTRACTING

Aldo Soldati was already considering a move out of the moribund Los Angeles Mafia scene when he discovered his ability to pop from one location to the next. He proceeded to pile up a war chest of fuck-you money through a series of teleport-enabled solo heists. Tiring of the hard and risky work this entailed, he came to mutant city to sign on with the only La Cosa Nostra crew head for whom genetic enhancements were a plus. Vetroni put him in charge of the Fiorillo family's languishing corrupt contracting empire, assigning him to goose the earnings from its shadow interests in construction and waste management firms. The mob makes its cut from these by skimming off the top, maintaining effective monopolies through intimidation and extortion.

Since joining Vetroni's crew, Soldati has grown fat and lazy. He rarely stirs from the comfy lounge chair in his swanky den, except to socialize and talk business with Vetroni and his fellow captains. Although he also runs the outfit's hijacking operations, he no longer goes on stick-up runs himself. His favorite activity is reviewing spreadsheets of his various off-shore accounts. Confident that his teleport ability will get him out of trouble if somebody comes to whack him, he takes liberties with his new boss he wouldn't have attempted back in L.A. Soldati's greed has led him to start shorting Vetroni's cut from the various enterprises under his control. If either the boss or Martelli noticed this long-running accounting error, Soldati's days would be numbered—if he didn't quickly wedge his bulky frame into the witness protection program.

Soldati sent out the guys who performed the dynamite truck hijacking: two transplanted cousins from Los Angeles, "Short" Vito Stefanelli and "Tall" Vito Cipriani.

AL "POPPER" SOLDATI

Athletics 1, Driving 2, Health 6, Scuffling 2, Shooting 2

Powers: Spatial Awareness 3, Teleport 12, Telekinesis 3

Al's layer of fat protects him against blades and gun fire; damage he takes from these weapons is halved.

SALVATORE "BOOM BOOM" SPIGGIA
NARCOTICS

Sal Spiggia sold drugs on the streets of Syracuse New York before his burgeoning mutant powers won him a ticket to the big show in the form of Jason Vetroni's fast-rising crew. Through his old connections he set up Vetroni's drug retail operation, buying from cocaine from Colombian cartels and heroin and ecstacy from the Russians.

He breaks these bulk shipments down into packages for sale in Mafia-dominated neighborhoods. Spiggia also acts as a one-stop middleman to street-level African-American and Latino drug gangs looking to retail a diversified slate of product. Recently he started supplying a barhead-run prison drug network, much to his secret amusement. Last month he got tired of hearing one of these clients talking trash about the gene-expressive, tracked him to a deserted parking lot, wrapped him in a bear hug and blew him up. The murder of this man, Johnny Schneider, 28, has gone unnoticed, except for the discovery of a scorched and as yet unidentified severed foot on top of a nearby convenience store. Sal has yet to mention this incident to any of his cronies. He's dying to brag about it and may do so when tipsy—possibly while the detectives are listening in.

Osvaldo Sanchez, one of Schneider's confederates, has just learned that the outfit they buy their coke and heroin from is riddled with mutants. Although his small band of barheads is scarcely equipped for a full-on war with a large Mafia family, Sanchez is not bright enough to see that and may start trouble that the squad can capitalize on.

Spiggia's acquisition of explosive powers may seem ironic, in that he earned his nickname prior to mutation, as an expert bomb maker. "Boom Boom" built and installed the bomb in Broadway Bob's car.

His biggest secret has nothing to do with dead barheads: having suffered for years in silence, he has recently begun taking prescribed anti-depressants.

SALVATORE "BOOM BOOM" SPIGGIA

Athletics 6, Driving 6, Health 8, Scuffling 6, Shooting 6

Powers: Analytic Taste 1, Self-Detonation 24, Suppress Explosion 6

Boom Boom is good at hiding from the cops. Surveillance difficulties to spot him are never less than 5.

PETER "SNAKES" GUIDELLI
PANDERING / HUMAN TRAFFICKING

"Snakes" Guidelli is one of two captains remaining from the old Fiorello mob. He was the first to throw in the towel and join up with Vetroni during his takeover. In the years since, he has come to bitterly regret his betrayal of the old crew. The more he sees of his new cohorts' mutant powers, the more sickened he becomes. He especially hates the fact that people now think *he's* a mutant. Based on his nickname, they assume he's a reptile and amphibian commander. He earned that name honestly, damn it, back in the days when it *meant* something for your buddies to call you "Snakes."

The rumor mill also says he can induce fear. Snakes is a terrifying figure, but he comes by that the old fashioned way. A tall, shovel-faced man, he uses his linebacker's physique to intimidate rivals, citizens—even cops. Guidelli runs a high-end prostitution ring. Other vice activities include collecting protection from street-level pimps and extorting strip clubs into purchasing his pricey security services. Snakes has branched out into people smuggling, running illegal aliens into mutant city. Some of the women he's been paid to sneak into the country wind up working in his prostitution business, not always voluntarily.

Snakes might cooperate with police if he thought it would help him retake the family for the genetically normal—with himself in charge, naturally.

Vetroni does not feel the personal affection for Guidelli he reserves for closer cronies, but respects his power as an earner. If he found out how much Guidelli despises him, he might preemptively put him in the ground.

PETER "SNAKES" GUIDELLI

Abilities: Athletics 8, Driving 4, Health 12, Scuffling 12, Shooting 12

JOHN CARBONI
EXTORTION

The family's other non-mutant captain, John Carboni, runs the family's protection racket. He continued the old guard's fight against Vetroni's power play even after the old boss was killed. After a sitdown sponsored by a mob leader from a nearby city, Carboni reluctantly agreed to accept Jason's leadership. The true burial of the hatchet occurred a year later, after the new boss became engaged to Carboni's niece, Anna. Vetroni became not just family, but *family*, and now Carboni won't hear a word against him.

Carboni is in his fifties, dresses modestly, and takes a low-key role at mob social events. He keeps a mistress on the side for propriety's sake but would still rather spend time with his demure wife, Doreen. Anna Vetroni's father died when she was young; John has done his best to serve as a substitute paternal figure, while also doting over his own children, Frank, 23, Mario, 21, Trina, 20, and Drina, 19. The two sons are following in Dad's footsteps, helping him out with lower-risk collections. Unfortunately, they're both hotheads who might be easily goaded into violence—perhaps by the detectives, looking for leverage over their father. John will expect them, if popped, to earn their stripes by serving their time with silent determination, but might change his tune if they're put under sufficient pressure.

HARD HELIX

JOHN CARBONI

Athletics 8, Driving 4, Health 12, Scuffling 12, Shooting 12

LOWER LEVEL GUYS

As the squad members are targeting the big fish, you will also probably need to describe lower level mob members that they encounter along the way. These additional figures are provided without affiliation, so you can insert them into scenes as needed. As your version of "The Vanishers" unfolds, you may decide to make Dominick Ninchi a runner for Paul Martelli, while another GM might use him as hijacker working for Snakes Guidelli.

Except where noted, the lower level guys all have the same game statistics. Naturally, you should alter these as needed to fit their role in your narrative.

LOWER LEVEL GUYS

Abilities: Athletics 4, Driving 4, Health 4, Scuffling 4, Shooting 4

DOMINICK NINCHI

Dominick Ninchi is a squat, portly young man with a fondness for vibrant, appallingly patterned sweaters. He regards himself as an up-and-comer in the Vetroni organization. Ninchi recently arrived from Vegas, having demonstrated to Jason his ability to shrug off incoming bullets. If a squad member infiltrates the gang, Dominick may view him as a mutant rival or a kindred spirit, depending on your dramatic requirements. On first impression, he seems dense but affable. When push comes to shove, Dominick is enough of a sociopath to commit any act of violence to get in good with Vetroni.

Dominick has yet to be assigned a colorful nickname and is anxious to acquire one as soon as possible.

DOMINICK NINCHI

Powers: Concussion Beam 12, Kinetic Energy Dispersal 12, Limb Extension 6

TOMMY "FLOWERS" FRERO

Tommy is a skinny, pug-faced guy known for yapping incessantly when nervous. He wears Hawaiian shirts as part of an elaborate strategy to make people think his nickname somehow derives from his clothing choices. In fact, it's a cutting reference to his record of prison homosexuality. Low-ranking squad members who refer to it too knowingly may suddenly find themselves facing down the barrel of his snub-nosed ankle piece.

JIMMY "THE WHEEL" MAGGIO

A white-haired, spectacularly obese holdover from the old days, Jimmy Maggio is kept in the saddle for his impeccable odds-making ability on sports betting, and for his implacable hand behind the wheel of any vehicle. Adopting a fatalistic attitude toward the criminal lifestyle, he's survived multiple turnovers in mob power by keeping his head down and his earnings up.

JIMMY "THE WHEEL" MAGGIO

Athletics 2, Driving 14, Health 2, Scuffling 2, Shooting 6

STEVE "STRIPES" MAZZONI

This former marine turned to the family crime business after a tour in the first Iraq War and a subsequent dishonorable discharge for crushing a fellow soldier's eye socket in a barroom brawl. Alternately taciturn and belligerent, Steve holds forth on politics at the drop of a hat. Although proudly reactionary, he's had to backpedal his anti-mutant views since Vetroni's ascendancy. He's now decided that certain mutants, like Jason, can win his respect by demonstrating a firm authority over the weak and stupid.

LENNY "PUPS" ALPHARETTA

If he weren't the nephew or cousin of an aforementioned Vetroni captain of your choice, this lackadaisical slacker and jokester wouldn't be trusted to carry a can of nails. As such, he's assigned simple, low-risk errands and allowed to play the role of group mascot. Mostly this means serving as a butt of jokes, which Lenny, happy to hang out with the big guns, takes in grinning stride. In a pinch, he might be sent to perform a job that gets him in over his head. Loose-lipped gang members have revealed way too much in his familiar presence. An undercover squad member might steer him into a jam that he can get out of only by turning state's witness. Very proud of his sartorial choices,

Lenny spends most of his spare scratch on fashionable new clothes.

DAVID "FRENCHY" ROAD

A rare non-Italian among the Vetroni mob, David Road knows he can't ascend to the top tier and is perfectly happy making a lucrative illegal living without involving himself in the dangers of mob politics. He's a ropy, sandy-haired guy who loves guns and enjoys extensive contacts in the outlaw biker scene. His nickname derives from his Montreal birthplace, even though he's actually the black sheep of an Anglo family.

TAKEDOWN

The dismantling of the Vetroni outfit might take exclusive focus for a number of sessions, or serve as a recurring element between other investigations. Let the players take the lead on deciding how to go about it. Their goal is to get enough information to sew Vetroni and crew up for the Broadway Bob scam and for their many much worse crimes. All of the characters in the previous section have at least one murder on their ledgers.

CONDUCTING INTERVIEWS

None of the underbosses dare talk to the cops for any extended period. They either stay tight-lipped or stick to crude insults, depending on their level of caution.

Jason, however, is egotistically invested in his ability to maintain the facade of a legitimate businessman. He agrees to talk to squad members, but only on his turf. Vetroni turns on the charm, hoping to figure out what the cops know from the content of their questions. He carefully deflects all potentially damning queries and does not crack when Interpersonal abilities are deployed against him.

However, he does expose himself in one potentially useful slip. If interviewed in the sandwich shop or boxing club, a TV blares on a set of brackets behind Jason as he talks. As the dialogue hits a lull, a Broadway Bob commercial pops up on the TV. (This happens even if Bob is dead—his heirs are still running his ads until they can devise a new way to market the business.) When Bob's grating delivery booms out through the TV speakers, Jason winces. Then the TV image breaks down into static until the commercial ends. **Anamorphology** suggests that he's just unconsciously used the Technokinesis ability.

MENTAL SURVEILLANCE

If he knows that the squad members are conducting unauthorized surveillance using their mental powers, Special Agent Lerner can't look the other way. He'll be forced to file criminal charges against them. He can't book them for crimes they successfully conceal from him, of course.

Given that he does have wiretap authorization, and that it has consistently failed, **Law** tells the group that they may be able to get a warrant to use invasive mental powers. To do this they must reasonably show that Vetroni has the Technokinesis power and is using it to circumvent authorized wiretap equipment. Then they can commence an above-board thought invasion— with all the dangers inherent in getting close enough to Vetroni to pull it off.

GOING UNDERCOVER

Squad members' mutant powers give them an entrée to Vetroni's inner circle that Lerner's task force lacks. They can build a case on him by infiltrating his organization. His mob is easier to penetrate than

HARD HELIX

other La Cosa Nostra groups because he recruits from elsewhere. Squad members working their way into his crew will still need to be vouched for by a connected guy, though.

Fortunately, Lerner can help, by arranging an introduction by Leo "Cubby" Cenci, a mob figure from Florida who has secretly turned state's witness. With Cenci acting as technical advisor, Lerner can produce credible criminal histories for up to two fake identities.

Vetroni tests the new recruits by giving them a series of illegal jobs to perform. These escalate gradually in seriousness, and degree of exposure they place him in. They might be required to:

- pick up a mysterious package from an unidentified guy who will meet them in a parking lot somewhere
- gently remind a recalcitrant debtor to pay up
- torch an abandoned building in an insurance scam
- collect from the previous debtor, no matter what
- whack a suspected informant

As these scenes unfold, ratchet up the pressure, making it progressively harder for the PCs to remain undercover without crossing the line.

They will be handed over to one of the captains (or two of them if there are two undercover officers), who will supervise their efforts. Vetroni makes these assignments based on the powers and skills the PCs claim. Someone with emotion control might be sent to help Snakes Guidelli keep his hookers in line. More physical powers place the cop in John Carboni's extortion ring. Depending on the scenes you improvise in response to player choices, they may learn enough on Vetroni to nail him directly. Or they might gather intel only on their captains, enabling them to flip them.

Check out the excellent 1997 film *Donnie Brasco*, featuring Johnny Depp and Al Pacino, as a source of inspiration for classic undercover-against-the-Mob situations.

As only a couple of PCs can plausibly engage in the undercover mission, you'll need to find interesting and exciting challenges for the rest of the squad. They might be engaged in parallel surveillance, mutant-powered or mundane. They could act as behind-the-scenes backup, helping to fake the undercover types' apparent crimes. Or they could pursue other cases while the undercover sequence unfolds as a B-story. (Make sure, though, that you don't deprive the group of investigative abilities they need by sending the undercover guys off on their own mission.)

A BIG FINISH?

As is often the case in Mutant City Blues, the climax of the case can be played out as a final super battle or in a non-violent arrest sequence. The former choice suits groups more attuned to the super side of the game, while the latter is more realistic and in keeping with the police procedural genre. For a super finish, the mobsters fight back when busted. In a procedural ending, they submit calmly to arrest, sure that expensive lawyers will do more for them than telekinetic attacks or self-detonations. Meanwhile, Sean Lerner and the squad members pop champagne corks, congratulating themselves on landing a landmark case.

RECOVERING THE JEWELS

While the squad tackles the Vetroni mob, they may either remain focused on their original entry point into the case—the Broadway Jewelry heist—or allow it to fade into the background.

As mentioned in the profile entry for Paul "the Lawyer" Martelli, he has custody of the jewels that disappeared from Broadway Bob's safe. They were taken from the store, under Border's supervision, the night before Soto's gang of patsies showed up. An examination of the jewels with **Streetwise** confirms that this batch of jewelry consists of easily fenced materials, where Soto was allowed to take only pieces too distinctive to unload on the black market.

The squad can tie up the loose ends on this aspect of the case either by getting the real story while undercover, or motivating a gang member to flip on the others.

CHARACTER QUICK REFERENCE

"Broadway" Bob Border – Jeweler and into the mob

Gabe Losey – Broadway Jewelry robber

Horace Monette – Broadway Jewelry robber

Cristina McGonagle – Broadway Jewelry robber

Alex Soto – Broadway Jewelry robber

Sarah Soto – Broadway Jewelry getaway driver

Georgiana Koenig – Sales clerk at Broadway Jewelry

Amy Ore – Sales clerk at Broadway Jewelry

Larry Evans – former football player, customer of Broadway Jewelry

Sean "Twan" Bridewell – drug dealer

("Grassy") – drug dealer

Ray Ashe - claims adjuster from Pacific Partners Insurance

Vivien Coleman – Broadway Bob's lawyer

John "Heck" Reid - bookie

S. A. Lin Mosswood - ATF Agent

(Dolph Delaughter) – hijacked truck driver

S.A. Shane Lerner - team leader of an anti-organized crime task force at the FBI

Jason "the Machine" Vetroni – Mutant mob boss

Anna Vetroni – wife of Jason Vetroni, step-daughter of John Carboni

Paul "The Lawyer" Martelli – Mob captain

Violetta Martelli - wife of Paul Martelli

Other Violetta – Paul Martelli's mistress

Paul Junior Martelli – Paul Martelli's son.

Chrissy – Paul Martelli's daughter

Danny "Flipper" De Filippo – mob captain

Al "Popper" Soldati – mob captain

"Short" Vito Stefanelli - mob hijacker

"Tall" Vito Cipriani – mob hijacker

Salvatore "Boom Boom" Spiggia - mob captain

(Johnny Schneider) – murdered Barhead

Osvaldo Sanchez - barhead druggie

Peter "Snakes" Guidelli – mob captain

John Carboni – mob captain

Doreen Carboni – wife of John Carboni

Frank Carboni – son of John Carboni

Mario Carboni – son of John Carboni

Trina Carboni – daughter of John Carboni

Drina Carboni – daughter of John Carboni

Dominick Ninchi – mob soldier

Tommy "Flowers" Frero – mob soldier

Jimmy "the Wheel" Maggio – mob soldier

Steve "Stripes" Mazzoni – mob soldier

Lenny "Pups" Alpharetta– mob soldier

David "Frenchy" Road– mob soldier

Leo "Cubby" Cenci – mobster-turned-informant

HARD HELIX

SUPER SQUAD

A sudden death at a mutant-related riot leads the unit into the twisted world of the Super Squad, an elite policing group who work the city's toughest streets—and have, in the process, gotten more than a little dirt on their own shoes.

BACKSTORY

Two years ago, police headquarters approved the formation of the SITF, or Street Interdiction Task Force. Led by hard-charging police detective Garth Marquez, the SITF enjoys wide latitude in the war against the city's drug gangs. It gets up close and personal with street-level criminals and their bosses, developing the force's best intel on gang activities. The task force runs confidential informants and sweeps drug corners. It launches lightning raids on crack dens, stash houses, meth labs, and money counting operations. If in the process, it leans a little too heavily on the skels, or racks up a few too many complaints for brutality or use of racially insensitive language—well, their results are so good that the top brass has found it in their interest to look the other way.

In the face of this oversight gap, the rough tactics of the Super Squad have metastasized into straight-up corruption. The SITF charges protection fees to favored gangs and busts their competition. They skim confiscated money and drugs, wholesaling stolen evidence to their gangsters of choice.

Last month, Marquez began to receive insinuating emails from an unknown source, threatening to expose his criminal activities if as-yet-unspecified financial demands were not met. A restless sleeper tormented by guilty dreams, Marquez came to realize that the information in the emails could only have come from a mutant eavesdropping on his nightmares. Conducting an investigation on his neighbors in his apartment complex, he zeroed in on Irwin Poling, the pale, bean pole of a man who living immediately above him.

THE CRIME

Marquez enlists his favored gang leader of the moment, Lamar Yancey, ordering him to kill Poling. Yancey shadows him to a downtown watering hole, where he enjoys a stroke of luck—a spontaneous anti-mutant riot has broken out across the street! Yancey murders Poling and drags his body a nearby parking lot, hoping that he'll be treated as a riot victim.

THE INVESTIGATION

The PCs are on the scene while the crime is committed, during the introductory action sequence **Riot In Helixtown**. In **Beamed Out**, they are led to the corpse and discover that Poling was killed by concussion beam. The **Sad Apartment Of Irwin Poling** leads them to the Marquez connection. In **The Neighbor**, they talk to Marquez and get the feeling that something's hinky about him. If they consult Internal Affairs, **Eating Cheese With the Rat Squad** suggests that Marquez is well-protected by the brass and can only be taken down with rock-solid evidence.

THE TWIST

Yancey isn't as cool a customer as Marquez; he panics and stages a **Drive-By** shooting on the PCs. They can catch and capture him but, in **No Snitching**, discover that he's not about to give up Marquez.

Immediately afterward, the squad finds itself dodging bureaucratic fire, as higher-ups pressure them to **Ease Off** and close the case with Yancey.

Then Yancey goes **Up In Smoke**, as an unidentified fellow prisoner kills him with spontaneous combustion.

In **The Big Skate**, creepy low-level dealer Jeff Bibby is suddenly freed from the same facility after evidence against him goes missing. **Chain Of Custody** leads the HCIU to property officer Michelle Mink. Another run at

Frank wins the trust of their IAD contact, who points them to Marquez's secret storage **Locker**. If they can work out a way to get inside and still use the contents as evidence—perhaps stepping onto Marquez's questionable side of the street—they discover an incriminating tape. In a follow-up interview, **Michelle Cracks**.

THE CULPRIT

Mink's promised testimony gives them the opening they need to commence the final **Showdown** against Marquez and his Super Squad. Despite their collective nickname, they're not enhanced—but their SWAT-level armaments make them the next best thing.

SCENES

RIOT IN HELIXTOWN

SCENE TYPE: ACTION TEASER

The action begins as the squad speeds to the scene of a potential riot in progress in Helixtown, the city neighborhood known for its high concentration of enhanced citizens. Due to their ongoing relationship to the community, they've been sent to the scene to try to calm the disturbance. The riot squad is on its way, but if the HCIU gets there first, they're to take action to prevent anyone from being hurt.

The street demonstration has jammed traffic over a several-block radius. Any PCs who have been driving to the scene must get out and walk the rest of the way, jostling their way through onlookers. (Fliers and teleporters, obviously, have ways of bypassing the crowd.) As they head to the epicenter of the disturbance—a sports bar called Nets—they navigate their way through a confused crowd spilling from the sidewalks. Some people are running from the scene: parents with young kids, elderly folks, ordinary citizens, all clearly fearful.

Others sprint toward the fray. Detectives with **Streetwise** identify some of the following. They include both notorious Helixtown troublemakers and known anti-mutant agitators. Each detective spots one skel for each point in his Streetwise pool; none of these IDs requires a spend. Make sure the group notes the

HARD HELIX

presence of at least one problem citizen from each side of the mutant divide.

Mutants known to police:

- Jimmy the Mope, a shiftless meth-head who uses Emotion Control to keep his abused girlfriend of the moment depressed and vulnerable to his head games.

- Tequila Encinas, a sometimes violent transvestite prostitute who lets her johns burn and cut her, later healing herself with Regeneration.

- Jonathan Lynch, a self-righteous, hot-headed activist who uses his Force Field to push people around.

Barheads and fellow travelers:

- Kenneth Westray, an insecure pretty boy who gets into fights with mutants to impress his bigoted girlfriend, Ana.

- Self-pitying cafeteria worker Nasim Iqbal, who scuffles with mutants as a way of releasing his sense of humiliation over his lowly employment status.

- Desiree Whitson, who drifted from the extreme animal rights movement to the Neutral Parity League after losing her husband to a green-skinned rival.

As you name these characters, the players may take notes, thinking that they'll end up as important suspects later. Do not disabuse them of this notion.

If players propose a credible-sounding way of discouraging any of these trouble hounds from joining the riot, assign appropriate Difficulty modifiers and let them have at it. Any single instigator can be warned away on a 1-point Law, Intimidation or Negotiation spend.

In front of Nets, fists and bats are already flying as two groups of citizens lay into each other. **Streetwise** users note more mutant and anti-mutant agitators among the crowd. Six or seven uniformed officers have retreated to their respective patrol cars. One holds a crimson-stained dishtowel to his battered head.

Trampled beneath scuffling feet lie several placards bearing a photograph of a man wearing football equipment, or such legends as JUSTICE FOR EDISON MULLAN or NOBODY PUTS HUMANS IN THE CORNER.

Trivia gets the reference. Edison Mullan, quarterback of the local football team, is in intensive care at the city's best hospital, after being clotheslined by a player on the other team. That player, David Harpe, has since confessed to having recently developed mutant Strength. Although Harpe has expressed his remorse and been forgiven by Mullan, a friend and former teammate, the incident has reawakened the controversy over the mutant role in professional sports. **Cop Talk** surmises (and uniformed officers can confirm) that a spontaneous protest started peacefully but was quickly escalated by opportunistic thugs on both sides.

(Feel free to change the details to another sport to suit your chosen city and the time of year in your game.)

The riot sequence is intended as an exciting opening scene in which the players get to creatively use their super powers to solve an open-ended problem. Allow any plausible plan to succeed, requiring rolls to deploy super powers as per usual.

Possible solutions you might anticipate include:

- using Emotion Control to bring calm to the violent

- using Endorphin Control (Others) to bliss out riot ringleaders

- Induce Fear on one or more ringleaders causes them to meekly cower before their opponents, demoralizing their supporters

- Illusions might send rioters fleeing

- Water blast mimics the power of a well-known anti-riot measure

Forensic Psychology allows the user to identify the two or three instigators on each side of the fight whose aggression motivates the rest to keep fighting. If they are neutralized, the crowd's mood reverses and the fighting de-escalates.

If possible, describe the scene so that PCs have to combine their power uses to quell the riot.

If the players are unable to solve the problem, the riot squad finally squeezes it way past stopped traffic to disperse the rioters with tear gas. Many, in fact, hightail it as soon as the heavily armored squad rolls up.

Whoever ends the riot, one of the uniformed officers calls out to detectives just as they're getting ready to depart. Behind the tavern, partially obscured behind a dumpster, lies the fatally beaten body of Irwin Poling.

BEAMED OUT
SCENE TYPE: CORE

The victim is a Caucasian male in his late fifties. He's tall and very thin. A pair of shattered eye glasses lies a few feet from his battered corpse. He wears brown corduroy slacks, a yellow polo shirt, badly worn brown suede loafers, and mismatched sports socks.

Forensic Anthropology suggests that he was killed by multiple blows from a blunt instrument of unknown type.

(core) **Energy Residue Analysis** shows that the blows that killed him were made by a concussion beam.

Evidence Collection spots blood spatter on the inside of the door leading from the bar outside to the dumpster area. Spots of blood also appear on the stairs, and are then pooled around the body. Overall they suggest that the vic was first hit inside, then again as he tried to escape down the stairs, and was hit multiple times while prone on the tarmac.

The door is marked FIRE EXIT ONLY but it isn't locked or alarmed.

The victim's wallet contains $60 in cash. Identification includes a debit card and driver's license, but no credit cards. From the driver's license the squad IDs him as Irwin James Poling. The address lists his residence as an apartment building in a downscale neighborhood. It's not in Helixtown, but in an adjoining area that hasn't seen the same level of gentrification.

Cop Talk confirms, if there was any doubt, that the squad has officially caught this case. They should check in with their lieutenant and inform support staff to get the usual paperwork rolling.

Inside the Net, the bar's small staff has already begun the process of picking up. Chairs have been toppled, and there are a few broken glasses, but by and large the bulk of the violence took place outside the bar. As the blood spatter says that the struggle began inside the bar, detectives may want to insist that the clean-up stop. (It turns out that there is no physical evidence of note inside, anyway.)

The owner/bartender is Carla Porter, a no-nonsense woman in her late forties sporting brassy-colored locks pulled back into a pony tail. She takes the lead in answering detectives' questions. Though not particularly hostile, Carla is more focused on cleaning up than on chewing the fat with the cops. The suggestion that she might be able to apply for damages as a crime victim, dangled via **Negotiation**, gets her full attention.

- She knew the victim to see him, but not by name. He came in infrequently, nursed a beer or two, and then left. She never saw him talk to other patrons or pay attention to the games on TV.

- He gave off the vibe of a man who wanted to be left to drink in peace, so she never quizzed him on his life or anything like that.

- If he had an opinion one way or another about mutants, she never heard it.

- As usual, he sat by himself in a small corner table near the fire exit.

- He seemed surprised and dismayed when the disturbance started. Once everything went crazy she stopped paying attention to him.

- The mix of patrons was the usual—about two-thirds regulars, one third people she didn't recognize.

- It's a mutant-heavy neighborhood, so of course a good percentage of the regulars are enhanced.

- Carla and her late husband started this bar long before the SME, when this was a slightly ragged working class neighborhood. The people have mostly turned over as it slowly turned into Helixtown, but they drink beer like anyone else. So long as you treat the place

HARD HELIX

with respect and pay your tab at the end of the night, Carla doesn't care what you've got in your mitochrondria.

- The trouble started when a loud table full of jerks started mouthing off about the Edison Mullan business. They were obviously out-of-towners, spoiling for a fight against the freaks.

- Of course some of the locals—Fast Freddy, Bob Harris, Lynette the Lightshow—took the bait and started arguing back.

- Maybe Carla could have contained it if she hadn't told them to take it outside. It seemed like there were more humps out there waiting to join the fight once the advance team had drawn some hotheads out onto the sidewalk.

- By the time the riot started, the whole staff, including Carla, was out there, too, trying to calm folks down. Nobody saw anything happen to Poling.

- There's a security camera in the back room, where she keeps the safe, but nothing pointed at the bar area itself. "People like to get their drink on without Big Brother watching their every move."

None of the other staff members have anything significant to add to Carla's account. **Bullshit Detector** shows that both she and her employees are playing it straight.

CANVASSING THE RIOTERS
SCENE TYPE: RED HERRING

A check with other local businesses show that a number of them keep cameras trained on the street. Incidents of vandalism are all too common in Helixtown. These are almost invariably perpetrated by barheads or out-of-town yahoos who pour into the district on weekends to gawk at the creeps and raise hell.

Data Retrieval searches the gathered video footage for an angle on the back of Nets, but comes up with nothing. However, it is easy to see who threw the first punches during the riot, and who escalated from fists to makeshift clubs and super powers.

TABLE OF JERKS

The table of jerks Carla described as instigating the fight are all plainly visible in the footage. **Data Retrieval** permits the use of facial recognition software to see if any of them are in the system. They get one hit: a thick-necked young gentleman named Tad Borman is in the database as a former army private. **Law** decodes the attached personnel record to show that he was dishonorably discharged after some kind of disciplinary incident while stationed in Korea.

Research finds an address for a Tad Borman in an aging suburb far from the city center.

Borman comes to the door of his house in socks, gym shorts and T-shirt. If it's an odd hour, he explains he's just gotten off shift as a cable installer. Evasive at first, he continually looks behind him into the house. **Reassurance** or **Negotiation**, suggesting that the detectives won't tell his wife about his involvement in the riot, secures his cooperation.

- Borman admits that he and a bunch of his dumb-ass high school buddies got together and decided to go ruffle some feathers in freaktown. His young son is a huge fan of Edison Mullan and he hated having to explain how a great player's career could be ruined because a mutant didn't reveal his status.

- (If none of the detectives are visibly enhanced, Tad blithely spouts anti-mutant slurs, as if expecting that any self-respecting cop would openly disdain the chromes. If they are, he nervously tries to speak in politically correct terms: "Don't get me wrong. Some of my best friends are differently genetic.")

- They never expected this to turn into a full-fledged riot. Once it happened, they got the hell out of there. [Surveillance footage confirms this.]

- Neither Borman nor any of his friends had any idea that there were a bunch of barheads milling around, ready to jump in and turn a simple bar rumble into world war three. They just wanted to let off steam.

Tad certainly doesn't know anything about any murder, and neither do his friends. They were together the whole time, and he can swear than none of them did anything worse than kick somebody in the nuts.

Bullshit Detector indicates that, though he may be shading the truth to make himself look like less of a loser, Borman is basically telling the truth.

Only if pressed will Borman give up the names and contact info for his friends: Joe Mahlum, Dustin Shepherd, Oscar Rosario, Danny Aube. If the detectives decide to question all of them, sum up the process in a quick sentence or two. They all independently confirm Tad's story, and exhibit varying degrees of contrition about their role in triggering a riot.

MUTANT BELLIGERENTS

Research allows the group to track down the group of mutants mentioned in Carla's account. Each requires a different means of approach and offers a slightly variant take on the same basic information.

Fast Freddy is Frederick John Rossum, 60, a professional gambler who clerks in a porn shop whenever he hits a losing streak. **Research** yields his minor rap sheet, including gambling and drug offenses and a string of assault charges. All of the latter stem from bar fights. He has never suffered a major conviction but fears that his involvement in the riot will provide his ticket to the pokey. On a 1-point **Research** spend, a detective can reach out to an arresting officer in the most recent case to learn that Rossum's powers are Speed, Reflexes, High Energy Dispersal, and Kinetic Energy Dispersal. Freddy is not enough of a hothead to get into a physical confrontation with police officers. **Intimidation** sees to it that his fear of not talking to the cops overcomes his fear of talking to the cops.

Trivia tells the group that Bob Harris, 41, sells model trains over the Internet and is a regular disturber of Helixtown community meetings. (1-point spend) A vocal eco-activist, Bob proudly announces his Environmental Awareness ability to nearly anyone who will listen. He's also well-known in the community as an accomplished eavesdropper, suggesting that he also has the Hearing power. (Bob also possesses Tracking and Olfactory Center but considers these less brag-worthy.) **Data Retrieval** uncovers his activities as a comment troll on global warming denialist blogs and forums.

Lynette the Lightshow is hard-drinking stripper Bridget Renaud, 24. A character with **Streetwise** has seen her locally famous act, in which she supplements her pole dancing with Illusion and Alter Form. After a few moments' interaction with her, a detective with **Forensic Psychology** suspects that she is in the early stages of multiple personality disorder, a defect appearing between her two known powers on the Quade Diagram. Indeed, Bridget talks about her stripper character as a separate person. She's most comfortable with men when they're acting like customers, and is attracted to strong women, so **Flirting** from either gender is a good way to open her up.

All three tell versions of the following story:

- They didn't start the riot. It was those stupid norms, fixing for a fight.

- They didn't like what happened to Edison Mullan anymore than anybody. He was a hometown hero.

- Nobody knew Irwin Poling, except to see him.

- They didn't notice him that night; they were to preoccupied with the table full of asshole norms.

- If he was killed, it's because some NPL thug thought he was a mutant. It had to have been a hate crime.

Once again, **Bullshit Detector** suggests that they're telling the truth, and that this line of inquiry is a dead end.

The mutant hotheads seen rushing toward the riot as the detectives arrived on scene have even less information, but share the opinion that Poling had to have been a mutant victim of an NPL hate crime.

BARHEADS

Surveillance footage of the riot shows Neutral Parity League youth wing leader Richard Wayne Jason (*Mutant City Blues*, p. 152) and two of his lieutenants, Tom Philson and Mike Griffin. Before Tad and his friends come out of the bar with Fast Freddy, Lynette the Lightshow and Bob Harris, the barheads seem to be loitering aimlessly around. They touch off the riot by suddenly jumping into the fray. Body language, as analyzed with **Forensic Psychology** or **Streetwise**, suggests that this was an unplanned, opportunistic gesture. **Streetwise** further suggests that they were down there looking for trouble.

Richard Jason agrees to speak with the detectives because he enjoys baiting mutant cops—especially this

HARD HELIX

time, when he doesn't feel he's done anything wrong. If the squad includes one or more non-mutants, Jason speaks only to them, trying to drive a wedge between the norms and the lixers. Tom Philson, a pathological sycophant, talks to the squad only if he's seen the big dog do it. Mike Griffin, if alone, yields to **Intimidation**.

Their story goes like this:

- They were just minding their own business, not looking for trouble with nobody.

- Yeah, so they, well-known mutant haters, were walking around in a gene-expressive neighborhood, wearing their gang insignia. What of it? It's a free country, isn't it?

- Sure, they jumped in when they saw honest citizens being menaced by mutant freaks. Any bar fight with them can turn deadly in a second, you know. Who can tell what kind of whacked-out powers they can unleash on your ass?

- They don't know no Irwin Poling.

- Obviously a mutant had to have killed him, probably because he was a pure genetic *homo sapiens* standing up for his innate rights. It had to have been a hate crime.

On a 1-point **Intimidation** spend (on Mike Griffin) or 1-point **Reassurance** spend (on Jason, from a non-mutant cop) or a 1-point **Negotiation** spend (on any of

SCOPING LAMAR

Scene Type: Alternate

Spends in the "Barheads" sub-scene may twig the detectives to the importance of Lamar Yancey, who does not otherwise appear until "Drive-By," See the ensuing section, "No Snitching", p. 52, for basics on Yancey's appearance and demeanor.

Depending on the order in which the detectives choose to follow their leads, this alternate scene may also provide their first introduction to Garth Marquez.

Cop Talk tells the group that the best source for drug intel is Marquez. They meet with him in his spartan office in a downtown police division. It is obviously little used: this is the setup of a guy who spends his time on the street and has been given a free pass on the paperwork. When Marquez first hears Yancey's name mentioned, he discourages the squad from seeking him out. Yancey is a very bad, trigger-happy guy, and an attempt to approach him could easily go wrong. He also (rightly) diminishes the relevance of NPL youth drug trafficking to their murder case. If pressed, Marquez agrees to set up a meet with Yancey, at which he and other members of his Super Squad will also be present.

Should a meet occur, it takes place on neutral ground, under a bridge. He comes with backup: one gangster for every squad member. Although their personal artillery is politely concealed, they are obviously strapped.

- Yancey, off the record, hints that he may have been in the vicinity to do business with the NPL.

- He doesn't care who is and isn't a mutant.

- He himself is not a mutant.

- He doesn't care about the riots. They do not impact on his business. He is a businessman.

- Jason is only a customer to him. When he's inside, Jason hangs with the Aryan Nation, which does not exactly endear him Lamar, an African-American.

Bullshit Detector on Yancey pegs him as an experienced player who maintains a perfect poker face at all times. It's impossible to tell when he's telling the truth and when he's lying.

If a player asks for a **Bullshit Detector** on Marquez, a 2-point spend allows them to see that there's something fishy between him and Yancey.

the three, with a promise to intercede with prosecutors regarding riot incitement charges they'll undoubtedly be facing), they confess that they were hoping to meet up with a gang contact to score a drug package. When they refuse to identify him, **Bullshit Detector** suggests that they're more afraid of the dealer than they are of the HCIU.

Coupled with the above spend, a 1-point **Streetwise** expenditure allows a detective to consult with a snitch who's wired into the local drug scene. (If you need a name and personality for the informant, use resourceful but paranoid junkie Devon Bullock.) He identifies the most likely source for Jason's drug activities as Lamar Yancey: see sidebar.

Local NPL leader Conrad Priestley (see *Mutant City Blues*, p. 151; also "The Hard Helix") would be very unhappy to hear that his youth lieutenant is back to dealing drugs again. If a squad member (preferably a token norm) pays him a visit to drop the word, a rift opens between the two men, which you can follow up on in a future scenario.

The anti-mutant bigots seen at the beginning of the riot sequence lack most of the above information, but volunteer the theory that Poling was a genetically pure victim of a mutant hate crime.

THE SAD APARTMENT OF IRWIN POLING

SCENE TYPE: CORE

Poling's address leads to a drab concrete low-rise apartment building. **Architecture** notes it as an anonymous 1960s structure in bad need of basic repairs.

Forensic Accounting explains this is a neighborhood where rents have gone down relative to inflation—as opposed to nearby Helixtown, where an influx of mutant residents, many of them well-heeled, has sent property values upwards. Many of the norms priced out of that area have relocated here.

Poling lives on the fourth floor. The sleepy-eyed superintendent, a grumpy transplanted German named Wolfgang Korn, lets them into the apartment. It's a one bedroom, furnished with worn and cast off pieces. The focus of the living room is a large salt water aquarium; **Natural History** identifies several prized species of coral. A search of the cabinet below the aquarium yields a stray receipt showing that he purchased supplies for it at Urban Reef, a specialty shop on the other side of town.

A computer mouse and printer sit on a wooden desk nearby. A cable modem rests on the floor below. There is space for a laptop but the machine itself is nowhere to be found.

Pay stubs for a company called MKC are haphazardly discarded into a desk drawer. A call to the phone number listed on the checks identifies it as a provider of business-to-business travel and logistics. Poling worked as a shipper in their local warehouse.

POLING'S LIFE

Clarissa Miles, manager of Urban Reef, remembers Poling as a regular but frugal customer. He would put animals on hold for a long time, carefully saving until he could afford them. Recently he hinted that his financial constraints were ending, and that he'd be able to quickly buy certain expensive fish and corals. Miles characterizes him as "slightly off", but suggests that eccentric customers are an occupational hazard in the aquarium business.

Marlene Bartholomew, Poling's supervisor at the warehouse, bluntly describes him as a "warm body" with low people skills.

A fellow worker, Gus Bruner, reveals that Irwin's nickname at work was "Mr. Pissy." He was always complaining about something, but over the past few months had undergone a sudden change in attitude. He'd become calmer and less aggrieved, though just as standoffish as ever.

Ruthie Yi, an attractive server at the coffee shop Poling frequents, says that he creeped her out, constantly staring at her. When he eventually asked her on a date, he looked like he was going to pass out from the anxiety. She turned him down as politely as she could, but he still got mad, telling he could look inside her, if he really wanted. From then on he'd avoid the place whenever she was on duty.

HARD HELIX

Also in the drawer is a newly issued passport. None of its pages are stamped. (Follow-up **Research** drawing on the international transport security network shows that he has yet to leave the country with it, and that he had gone for over a decade without renewing his previous, expired passport.)

Poling's bookshelves contain the occasional best seller and computer instruction manual, but are mostly filled with books on fish and aquariums. A guide book on travel to Africa lies open on an end table, to a page detailing tours in Malawi for tropical fish fanciers.

Coffee cups from the franchise café outlet down the street from his apartment fill his recycling bin.

Korn has a high opinion of Poling, in that he minded his own business, never bounced a check, and didn't bother people with a lot of pointless conversation.

(core) As they're leaving the building, the squad passes Garth Marquez, jingling his keys as he heads for the elevator. **Cop Talk** identifies him, if they haven't encountered him yet, as the detective in charge of the Super Squad.

Marquez is a tall, lanky man who walks with a confident macho swagger. He keeps his hair long, completing his quasi-bandido look with an elaborate mustache. Tight jeans, tighter black T-shirt, alligator-skin cowboy boots, and a skull-and-crossbones belt buckle complete the ensemble. He chain-chews toothpicks; a nicotine patch adorns his well-muscled forearm.

THE NEIGHBOR
SCENE TYPE: CORE

As longstanding police officers, squad members should already know a good deal about Marquez and his crew. If the players ask to draw on this presumed backgroundl knowledge of Marquez and his crew, supply the following facts. Try as much as possible to sound like you're making them up off the top of your head. Don't supply this information without prompting; that's too big a tell.

- He heads the SITF (Street Interdiction Task Force), tasked to perform high risk operations against the city's toughest street gangs.

- Its aggressive tactics have led to a sterling arrest record, including the roll-up of three major street gangs.

- These tactics balance sharp-elbowed raids and sweeps with extensive intel gathering. If you want to know what's up in the gang world, Marquez is your go-to guy.

- The city's right-leaning papers celebrate Marquez; the lefty rags accuse him of civil rights violations.

- Crooks claim he's dirty, but they say that about any cop they fear. [A character whose background includes a stint in Internal Affairs may have a more jaundiced view of Marquez and the Super Squad, suspecting that there's fire to go with that smoke.]

- Despite its name, none of the members are known to possess mutant powers. One of them is a Category B, though.

Marquez immediately makes the PCs as HCIU but pretends otherwise. When they call out to him, he takes a moment to recognize them, then greets them with the macho good-naturedness of a fellow officer.

(core) Although an accomplished liar, Garth has been practicing for this moment a bit too long, and pings **Bullshit Detector** when he pretends to be completely unaware of Irwin Poling.

If shown a photo, he frowns and thinks he's maybe seen him in the halls a few times. "I only crash here, man. Six months I been living here, and I still haven't unpacked the silverware."

He does not point out that his apartment is directly below Poling's, but doesn't lie about the location of his place if asked. He's in 309; Poling, in 409.

Marquez observes that Poling "looks like a citizen" and says he isn't on his radar.

If the group has heard of, but not gone looking for, Lamar Yancey, Marquez can now run the scene where he reluctantly agrees to arrange a meet; see sidebar, p. 46.

EATING CHEESE WITH THE RAT SQUAD

SCENE TYPE: ALTERNATE

When asking fellow cops about Marquez, the PCs must tread carefully—especially since all they have to go on is feeling that the SITF honcho is hiding something. Marquez is genuinely popular among rank-and-file cops. Mid-level managers sense that he's protected by somebody far up on the food chain. Any suspicion that the HCIU is looking into a fellow officer results in immediate and none-too-subtle pressure to back off—to prove that they're not doing the rat squad's job for them.

They'll probably think of it themselves, but if not, repeated references to the rat squad should inspire them to check out Marquez's rep within Internal Affairs.

The PC with the highest **Cop Talk** pool (resolve ties in favor of the player most in need of spotlight time) once served with an officer who joined Internal Affairs after repeatedly being turned down for deserved promotions. His name is Frank Williams.

Cop Talk tells them that even being seen entering the Internal Affairs department or seeking out an IAD investigator will result in a freeze-out from fellow officers. Being branded as a snitch or rat squad wannabe might deny them promotion, investigative cooperation, and even life-saving backup.

Let the players tell you how they plan to arrange for a secure meet with Williams. Then play out the logistical

RHINO IS WATCHING

In a prelude to the upcoming antagonist reaction, one of the obstacles to an unobtrusive IAD meet comes in the form of surveillance from Lamar Yancey's crew. When driving to the meet (adjust details as necessary based on player planning) a Difficulty 5 Sense Trouble check notices that the group's vehicle is being shadowed by a sleek late-model SUV. When the PCs appear to react, the vehicle speeds off. By winning a Driving vs. Driving contest (with Rhino Gomez at the wheel for the gangster crew) the PCs can intercept their vehicle and confront its inhabitants.

Rhino Gomez does the talking. He's a bulky guy with a congenital bump the size of a quarter in the middle of his forehead. Rhino denies that he was following anybody. He denies knowing Lamar Yancey. In fact, he denies everything.

The others are: Little Rex (Ray Henderson, a rangy fifteen-year-old), Sparks (De Andre Byrd, sullen and uncommunicative) and Ennis Anthony (tubby, a smart-ass.)

Without Yancey egging them on, these guys have no desire to get into trouble. If arrested, they go calmly along. Charges are unlikely to stick. There are no illegal weapons or drugs in the car.

Game statistics for Rhino and company are found in "Drive-By," p. 69.

Later **Research** shows that all inhabitants of the car have criminal records, including drug charges. All files note that they are subjects of an ongoing SITF investigation.

HARD HELIX

details, placing a few suspenseful obstacles in their path; see sidebar.

Frank Williams a straight-arrow guy who sports a severe hair cut, boasts a golfer's physique, and dresses like an FBI agent. He believes in his job, and is ruefully aware of the risks the squad is taking by nosing around another cop's business.

Frank starts by warning them off: "You don't want to go there, believe me." When pressed, he heaves his shoulders and drops a few more hints. Make the group work to drag even these tiny admissions from him.

- He was looking at the SITF last year, but closed the file, on orders from above.

- Even his own IAD bosses regard Marquez as untouchable.

- It's not that they're corrupt; it's that Marquez's work is too good to check. Three major gang roll-ups is nothing to sneeze at.

- To force his bosses to let him take a real run at Marquez, Frank needs something major. A few bundles of cash going astray—even a modest quantity of stolen drugs—won't cut it.

DRIVE-BY

SCENE TYPE: ANTAGONIST REACTION

After their the investigation hits the wall created by Marquez's juice within the department, the squad encounters a break in the case—courtesy of Lamar Yancey's drug-fueled paranoia.

Decide how Yancey knows which cops are working the Poling murder. He may have been tipped off by street contacts the PCs interviewed, by Richard Jason, or by a loose-lipped SITF member (other than Marquez.)

By default, the attempted hit occurs when squad members are traveling between scenes, preferably by vehicle. Otherwise it may happen while they are grouped together, on foot.

Lamar sits in the passenger's seat of the black SUV the team may have seen earlier in the "Rhino Is Watching" sub-sequence. Rhino is driving; the other gangsters previously referenced have jammed themselves into the back seat. Lamar sprays the group with automatic fire from a Mac-10 submachine gun.

Everybody except for Rhino disguises his appearance with a hoodie and a cheap plastic Halloween mask. Lamar's is a *V For Vigilante*-style Guy Fawkes mask; he is unaware of its various cultural resonances. Rhino, who has to drive, relies on a bandanna to hide his facial features. Since "Rhino Is Watching", they've switched the plates on their SUV for a set stolen from an ice cream truck.

Lamar stages the ambush effectively, roaring out of traffic at an unexpected moment. Seeing him coming before he fires requires a Difficulty 7 Sense Trouble test. If Lamar has met the PCs, he targets the one who got in his face the most. Otherwise, he aims for the driver (if the squad is in a moving vehicle) or the investigator who made the toughest impression on whoever told Lamar about them.

If the group is surprised, Lamar goes first. On a Sense Trouble success, the character making the test acts first, then Lamar, then the other PCs, then the gangsters in the back seat.

Their intention is to blast a cop or two quickly, then drive off. PC actions may prevent them from hitting in the first place, and will probably result in their capture. Characters in moving vehicles have their Hit Thresholds increase by 1. Lamar spends 3 Shooting on his first shot. If he hits, he uses his gun's autofire capacity: he spends all of his remaining Shooting points to do three additional instances of damage to him. Yancey, a closeted mutant, does not use his concussion beam powers unless his life seems to literally depend on it.

OPTIONAL RULE: AUTOMATIC WEAPONS

To keep the story moving and its main characters alive at least until the climax arrives, the action genre treats automatic weapons fire as much less deadly than it is in real life. Characters either remain pinned down by suppressing fire (which is realistic) or routinely outrun lines of machine gun fire (which is not.) Important characters are much less likely to be hit by automatic fire than they are by single firearm shots. Minor thugs, guards and henchmen are more likely to be hit by autofire.

The following optional rules allow for a more detailed treatment of automatic fire. It still models genre, not reality.

If you score a hit with an automatic weapon, and the GM has no narrative reason to prevent you from making an easy kill, you may then spend Shooting points to do additional instances of damage to him, at a rate of 1 instance of damage per 2 Shooting points spent. Damage is assessed after you decide how many extra instances you want to pay for.

Blake, raiding the compound of a Miami narco kingpin, uses a light automatic weapon to opens fire on a guard. He makes a Shooting test against his Hit Threshold of 3, spending 2 points to augment his roll. He rolls a 5, overcoming the Hit Threshold. Blake's player, Alex, decides to spend 4 points to purchase another two instances of damage. He now rolls three damage dice, getting a 5, a 3, and a 6, reducing the guard's Health by a total of 14 points. This takes the guard from 2 to -12 Health, leaving him dead. Blake has paid a total of 6 Shooting points for the entire exchange, taking his Shooting from 21 to 15.

If additional dramatically unimportant enemies stand within 3 meters of your first target, you may spread out your additional instances of damage between these additional targets.

Blake bursts through a door and finds the kingpin cowering behind a sofa, with three submachine gun toting goons waiting in front of it, shoulder to shoulder. Alex makes a Shooting test against the middle goon's Hit Threshold of 3. He spends 1 point on the test, rolls a 4, and hits. He may now pay 2 points apiece to do additional instances of damage to his initial target, or to the guys standing on either side of him. With 14 shooting points left, Alex chooses to hit each of them twice. Having already scored the first hit, the remaining five cost him a total of 10 points. He rolls three pairs of damage dice, getting a 3 and a 5 against his main target, a 3 and a 5 against the guy on the left, and a 5 and a 2 against the guy on the right. Each goon had 2 Health. Now the main target and guy on the left are both at -6 (seriously wounded), and the guy on the right is hurt, at -5 Health. The GM rolls Consciousness rolls for all three, failing each time. They all pass out, bleeding out on the palazzo's fine marble flooring.

HARD HELIX

DRIVING AND FIRING

To combine a ranged weapon battle with a driving contest, conduct a full round of combat between all eligible participants. At the end of the round, have each driver make his Driving test.

Hit Thresholds of characters in moving vehicles increase by 1.

Drivers may take a combat turn, but the Difficulties of Driving rolls and enemy Hit Thresholds increase by 2 apiece if they choose to do so.

If the pursuing driver fails, the combat ends prematurely as the lead vehicle speeds off, allowing its occupants to disengage from the fight.

If the fleeing driver fails, the vehicle spins out, crashes, or otherwise comes to a sudden stop. The chase has ended, but the combat may proceed. Combatants may hunker down in their vehicles to exchange further fire, or might elect to pile out and engage in close quarters fighting.

Losing a Driving contest during a fight usually results in a dramatic and hazardous crash. All occupants of the losing driver's vehicle make Athletics tests against a Difficulty of 4+x, where x is the difference between the Driving Difficulty (usually 4) and the driver's final result. Characters failing the Athletics test take one instance of unmodified damage.

LAMAR YANCEY

Athletics 6, Fleeing 6, Health 12, Scuffling 4, Shooting 12

Powers: Concussion Beam 12

Weapon: Mac-10 +2

RHINO GOMEZ

Athletics 8, Fleeing 2, Health 8, Scuffling 8, Shooting 4

Weapon: 9mm pistol +1

LITTLE REX, SPARKS & ANTHONY

Athletics 2, Fleeing 6, Health 2, Scuffling 4, Shooting 2

Weapon: 9mm pistol +1

None of these guys fights to the death. Unless they obviously have the upper hand when the PCs catch up with them, they throw down their weapons and surrender.

Lamar and company will probably be apprehended here. If so, go to "No Snitching." If not, go to "Hunting Lamar." If Lamar is killed, go to "Mourning Lamar."

NO SNITCHING
SCENE TYPE: CORE

Yancey and his crew remain tight-lipped under interrogation. Having committed a blatant attack on police officers in the line of duty, it's clear that they're all going away for a long time, even if the squad is unable to connect them to the Poling murder.

After a few moments with Rhino, Little Rex, Sparks or Anthony, **Streetwise** shows that they're not going to talk at all. The code of the street is too deeply ingrained in them.

The other gangsters use nine millimeter pistols and are incapable of autofire. Rhino does not shoot and drive but may use his weapon in the aftermath of a lost driving test.

How the scene resolves depends on player choice. A Driving and Firing sequence (see sidebar) is the most likely outcome. PCs with blast powers will probably be using them instead of firearms. Creative use of powers like force field, flight or technokinesis may allow the group to end matters in other ways.

A quick first impression of Lamar with **Forensic Psychology** suggests that his authority issues might trip him up. If there's a fact or detail he's concentrating on keeping under wraps, he can't be persuaded or tricked into giving it up. But he might be goaded into revealing secondary information the squad can use to build its case.

Giving Lamar the once-over with **Forensic Anthropology** points to the telltale signs of a multi-month cocaine binge. The paranoia this would have fueled undoubtedly inspired the bonehead move of attacking a group of police detectives.

In the interview, Lamar remains cocky, as if he's sure that he has a "get out of jail free" card.

- He shows vicious contempt for Marquez (which he genuinely feels; the man is shaking him down) while denying any dealings with him.

- Lamar denies knowing anything about Poling, or having any beef with him. (True, sort of.)

- He certainly didn't kill Poling. (False.)

- He says he attacked the squad because he "mistook them for someone else." He refuses to identify his supposed targets, except to say that they're business competitors of his.

The above distinctions between truths and falsehoods are provided for your reference only. **Bullshit Detector** shows that Lamar is mixing lies and facts but can't pin down which is which.

(core) PCs can use his authority issues and cocaine-damaged mental state to provoke an admission in kind. **Intimidation**, if accompanied with mockery and belittling, prompts him to use his concussion beam against his tormentor.

Whether he hits a detective or instead puts a dent in the interrogation room wall, **Energy Residue Analysis** can then match the distinctive edge of Lamar's concussion beam with the injuries on Irwin Poling's body. This allows them to book him on Poling's murder.

Now that they know to look for him, a **Data Retrieval** search of surveillance footage turns up an image of Lamar entering Nets prior to the riot. Witnesses previously canvassed at the scene, including Nets barkeep Carla Porter, ID him from a photo array as having been in the bar when everything went crazy.

If this occurs, their lieutenant congratulates them on closing another case. However, **Cop Talk** tells them that there's more to the story. **Law** further indicates that the district attorney will expect some follow up, especially regarding motive. They have plenty of physical evidence, but juries sometimes acquit if the prosecution can't explain why defendants committed the crime.

> ### WHAT LAMAR'S NOT TELLING
>
> Lamar goes to his grave with the following information, but it may come out during the denouement, either from Marquez or (more likely) one of his SITF confidants.
>
> - He is Marquez' handpicked drug lord. In exchange for warnings about prosecutions and shakedowns of rivals, Lamar gives the SITF a taste of his take, supplies information on his rivals, keeps the murders to a minimum, and stays out of the headlines.
>
> - Marquez saw him use his concussion beam years ago, when he was just another corner boy. Not even members of his own crew know this about him.
>
> - Marquez came to him demanding a murder as the price for keeping the deal going. He told Lamar to use his beam power, so Poling's death wouldn't look like a gang thing.

HUNTING LAMAR
SCENE TYPE: ALTERNATE

If Lamar gets away from the scene after his drive-by attempt, the squad finds him suddenly easy to locate. Word spreads through the drug underground that Yancey has committed a disastrous blunder that will eventually lead to his arrest. Rivals cease fearing him. Wanting him quickly out of the way so they can get down to the business of carving up his territory, they let the corner boys and junkies know that it's now

HARD HELIX

acceptable to tell tales on him. A canvass of city drug zones with **Streetwise** yields a location for Lamar's safe house. He's hiding out in a disused rail yard in an industrial zone.

When eventually found, Lamar and his crew are uncomfortably chilling in an old shipping container, outfitted with bedrolls, coolers full of beer, a portable DVD player, and a few other essentials.

The PCs can either make the raid on the rail yard themselves—allowing for a second action showdown against Lamar and his crew—or request a SWAT operation. Making a request through channels either for backup or a SWAT operation sends word filtering back to Marquez. He approaches the squad offering the services of the SITF. Garth insists on handling the whole raid himself, leaving the squad outside the yard, at a safe distance from the firing. A player calling on **Bullshit Detector** sees that Marquez is running an angle and is not to be trusted.

Should they rebuff him, Marquez catches wind of their plans to bust Yancey. His patrons in the department reach out to their lieutenant, demanding that the SITF be allowed to handle it. A dramatic scene ensues, in which the squad struggles to convince their lieutenant to take the political risk involved in keeping Marquez out. On a 2-point Cop Talk spend, their argument works without further repercussion. Without it, they're left with the impression that they've used up a big chunk of their brownie points with the boss and will one day have to repay him or her in kind.

If SWAT takes Lamar down, his capture occurs offstage, without incident.

If Marquez goes in, Lamar is—surprise, surprise—killed in the arrest attempt. Marquez' team members attest that it was a righteous shoot.

It's possible that the team will arrange to go in with Marquez. He attempts to maneuver himself into a position where he can execute Lamar without being caught. Stage the scene so that the team has a chance to see him trying and stop him from following through.

In situations where Lamar might be killed—either because the takedown occurs onstage, or because the SITF is going in alone—Rhino is not present during the arrest. This allows a fallback thread to fall into place in the event of Lamar's death: see "Mourning Lamar."

MOURNING LAMAR
SCENE TYPE: ALTERNATE

If Lamar is killed during an attempt to capture him, Rhino Gomez takes his place as the suspect who knows too much and gets crisped in prison during "Up In Smoke." In this case, he is the only member of Lamar's crew who knows the information given in the "What Lamar's Not Telling" sidebar on p. 53.

EASE OFF
SCENE TYPE: ANTAGONIST REACTION

With Lamar in prison and a sense of unresolved questions hanging over the case, the PCs may continue to take a run at the case. If they come at Marquez again, or try to talk to other members of the Super Squad (see sidebar), they get a reaction, in the form of political pressure from above.

The first approach comes from the lieutenant, who (possibly for the second time) urges them to wrap the case and move on. The boss reluctantly relents in response to a passionate argument.

Then a squad member (pick either the most aggressive questioner of an SITFer, or a player in need of spotlight time) finds his locker defaced and filled with small pellets of dried animal feces. **Natural History** identifies these as rat droppings—an unmistakable signal from the team's colleagues. Efforts to discover the vandal's identity merely increase the palpable animosity directed toward them.

Finally, assistant to the chief of detectives Adam Hemphill confronts them in the lieutenant's office, demanding that they lay out their evidence against Marquez. Give the impression that he's fishing for information. At the end of the meeting, he "strongly suggests" that they either drop the case or turn it over to Internal Affairs. **Cop Talk** tells them that it will go nowhere unless they get something Frank Williams can use. On a 1-point **Cop Talk** spend, a character recalls that Hemphill is a golfing buddy of Watch Commander Jonah Smith, uncle to SITF member Shawna Smith.

UP IN SMOKE
SCENE TYPE: CORE

When the "blue wall" theme of the previous scene appears to peak, the lieutenant gives them a piece of fresh news: Lamar Yancey has just been killed in jail.

MARQUEZ'S CREW

A tight bond of loyalty seals the SITF together—coupled with the knowledge that if one of them goes down, so do the rest.

Eusebio "U-Boat" Chavez is a young, hulking man of simple pleasures. He likes beer, strippers, professional sports, video games, and his gigantic home theater system, roughly in that order. This grinning jarhead delights in any opportunity to wreak mayhem on perps or scumbags. An unquestioning follower of alpha dog Marquez, he doesn't much trouble himself with the morality of the crew's corrupt practices. The team's least accomplished liar, U-Boat will wildly trigger **Bullshit Detector** if queried about the Poling murder.

The group's resident techie and gun wrangler, **Ray "Colley" Collins**, is the team's senior member. Marquez began as his protégé. Collins now happily acts as a combination of sidekick and voice of reason. A regular attendee of Gamblers Anonymous, Colley is still paying off a massive debt to several local bookies. Without the skim the squad takes from its busts, Collins would be dead meat. Colley won't talk, but a 1-point **Streetwise** spend points to the tics and jargon of the degenerate gambler.

A gentle soul who feels he owes Marquez his life, **Dominick Elder** guiltily dispenses his ill-gotten gains to a series of Catholic charities. He and Garth were foot patrolmen together. Marquez gunned down a convenience store robber who had already shot Elder twice and was about to put a round in his skull. Elder rationalizes the group's corruption by leaving the money alone and reminding himself of its stellar arrest record. He regards his personal debt to Garth as greater than his abstract obligation to the force, or to society in general. Dom clams up except in the face of **Reassurance**—in which case he tries to convince these nice cops to stay clear of the whole matter, for their own good.

Gung-ho policewoman **Shawna Smith** had to win acceptance from an unwilling team when top brass, including her high-ranking uncle, forced her on Marquez two years ago. She proved herself as willing to take crazier risks than anyone. He took a gamble and let her in on the team's corrupt side, which she has also enthusiastically embraced. She argues that if narcotics officers were paid on commission, there'd be a lot fewer dealers on the street. Shawna is an Anna May, a category-B mutant with the eerily enlarged eyes of a cartoon character. Her insecurity over this genetic deformity may account for her unstinting desire to prove herself to a group that didn't want her. Shawna would sooner submit to torture than give up this hardwon acceptance, but may enter into a tumultuous, ill-advised affair with a PC making a 2-point **Flirting** spend.

Game statistics for the SITF appear in "Showdown," p. 60.

Yancey was in the city's short-term holding facility awaiting arraignment. The corpse is in storage at the jail morgue. On arrival, the detectives are required to surrender their guns and escorted to the morgue by assistant warden Travis Brakkee, a blandly handsome man who interacts with them in a clipped, officious manner.

Yancey's severely charred corpse lies beneath a sheet on a metal table. The jail has no medical examiner; the body will be shipped to police forensic labs for further examination as soon as the detectives authorize the transfer.

Evidence Residue Analysis shows that Yancey was cooked from the inside out. His heart was set on fire from the inside. Burning flesh ignited his prison blues, which ignited and are responsible for the overall charring. The destruction of heart tissue implies a nearly instantaneous death.

Brakkee provides the following answers to specific questions:

HARD HELIX

- Yancey died in the cafeteria, in the presence of many guards and most of the jail's current population.

- Correctional officers reported no disciplinary problems with Yancey, including conflicts with other inmates.

- None of the guards saw him ignited, or found any lighters or accelerants on the prisoners, all of whom were searched before being allowed to return to their cells.

- Aside from a couple Category-Bs, none of the prisoners are listed in their dossiers as being mutants.

(core) Interviews with the many prisoners and guards present during the incident are mostly fruitless. **Bullshit Detector:** one of the inmates, Jeff Bibby, seems strangely smug when questioned. He's short, slightly cross-eyed, and speaks with a lazy drawl. Bibby remains calm if pressed, like he knows something the detectives don't.

Brakkee, if asked, supplies a visitor's list for Bibby. It includes two people: his lawyer, and his arresting officer, SITF member Shawna Smith.

If the team goes on to confront Smith about this, she says she was trying to flip him against his suppliers.

THE BIG SKATE
SCENE TYPE: CORE

Back at HQ, **Cop Talk** allows the group to access Bibby's rap sheet and court records. He appears to be a career criminal, with a range of petty crimes to his credit ranging from pimping to auto theft. His most recent arrest was logged by SITF detective Colley Collins, who caught him with a baggie of ecstasy pills.

(core) While they're looking into his case, they discover that Bibby has been suddenly kicked loose from jail, all charges dropped. (Find a natural way to bring this to their attention.) A call to the prosecutor on the case, ADA Lucille King, yields an explanation. Somebody screwed up in the police property department; the bag of pills has gone missing.

A visit to the basement apartment that is Bibby's recorded address shows that he's skipped town, subletting his place to a passing acquaintance, massage parlor worker Chloe Dunkin. In exchange for future consideration should she run afoul of the vice squad (**Negotiation**) Dunkin tells them that a big young guy with a bald head gave him a lift to the train station. Chloe won't say this on the record, because the guy gave off a cop vibe and she doesn't want to be making no cops mad at her. Shown a photograph of U-Boat Chavez, she quietly nods—and reiterates that she'll deny everything if they subpoena her.

CHAIN OF CUSTODY
SCENE TYPE: CORE

A trip to the police property office reminds the group of its sudden unpopularity. After they pass by, other cops make rat noises at them—stopping and adopting fake-innocent expressions when they turn around to see who's doing it.

The officer in charge of the property department, Sergeant Ralph Barbieri, is openly hostile to them. "You should be looking into perps, not cops." **Bureaucracy** reminds him of the procedural hassles they'll be able to inflict on him if he doesn't provide a few simple facts.

After reiterating that the disappearance of the pills has to be an administrative screw-up and not an act of criminal obstruction, Barbieri explains the following:

- Drugs and guns are more heavily secured than other pieces of evidence.

- The key to the locker has to be signed out. You also have to list a case number and file an electronic report justifying your access to the locker—either to place evidence in it, or to take it out for transfer to court or the custody of an investigator.

- Only property department officers are allowed near them. None of the SITF guys would be allowed to waltz in and access the locker.

(Barbieri is mostly telling the detectives, but not the players, what they already know.)

Forensic Accounting: An examination of the sign-out records from the time of Yancey's arrest to Bibby's release shows one anomalous entry. The case file number in the justification form refers to an already-closed prosecution.

This entry was made by Officer Michelle Mink.

A 1-point **Bureaucracy** spend secures secret access to Mink's personnel file. She was transferred to the property department, a dead-end assignment, after racking up too many citizen complaints as a foot patroller.

Mink, a skinny woman with straggly, unkempt hair, denies everything, in a demeanor of dull-eyed disinterest. She claims she made a simple data entry mistake. Jeff Bibby means nothing to her; she's never even heard of the guy. Like any property officer, she's logged lots of evidence submitted by the SITF but has no special relationship with any of them. This story does not pass the **Bullshit Detector** test, but she sticks to it.

THE LOCKER
SCENE TYPE: CORE

Now that they have reason to believe that Marquez played a role in two murders, but still have no solid evidence to crack the case, the detectives will probably pick up an earlier hint and take another run at IAD officer Frank Williams.

When they convincingly connect the dots for him, Frank reveals a piece of the puzzle he's been sitting on for months. Last year, he followed Marquez to a self-storage facility on the city's distant outskirts. He then found that Marquez rented a unit there under an assumed name. Department regulations forbid narcotics officers from holding any assets under concealed identities. However, given the pressure from superiors he faced after previous attempts to go after the SITF, Williams knew that it was too risky to bust him on a mere internal regulation. He decided to keep this card in reserve, playing it only when he had reason to believe that the evidence inside might implicate him in serious wrongdoing.

Williams provides the location of Marquez's secret storage unit, which is listed under the name of Frank Flintstone—Garth's contemptuous name for him. He gives them the signed affidavit they need to secure a search warrant on the locker. (**Law** explains why this is possible: narcotics officers waive their right to protection from search and seizure when they sign on for that duty.)

If players wonder why Williams isn't coming along on the raid, **Bureaucracy** supplies the answer. He's clearly insulating himself from the political risk if the squad goes after Marquez and comes up empty-handed. It's the PCs who will feel the brunt if they search his locker and then can't make the case.

At the storage facility, detectives deal with its owner, a wheezing, obviously unwell man named Vincent Nikula. He reacts to the search warrant with bored resignation, reminding them that the company he works for takes no legal responsibility for the contents of user's lockers. Shown pictures of SITF members, he identifies Marquez as the man who rents the locker, and Colley Collins as somebody he's seen with him. He does not recognize U-Boat, Dominick, or Shawna.

Banker's boxes, stacked along one wall nearly to the ceiling, contain unauthorized copies of case files Marquez has worked. Video tapes, DVDs, and

HARD HELIX

> ### OTHER SCENE ORDERS
> Frank's storage locker revelation can occur at any natural point after the death of Lamar Yancey. For example, the detectives might make a convincing case to Williams after Bibby skates. They might find the contents of the secret locker, and then, after watching the crackhouse blackmail tape, identify Michelle Mink as its subject when they go to the property department.

thumb drives are scattered across a battered wooden shelving unit. Assorted goodies are piled along another wall: a flat-screen TV, several sets of golf clubs, some expensive tire rims, and several cases of high-end Scotch. Several pieces of electronic equipment are stacked on a table, but only one of them is plugged in: a VHS-to-DVD copying unit. The locker contains no drugs or money; Marquez circulates that back into the system quickly, laundering the proceeds into a series of offshore accounts.

(core) **Evidence Collection** notes that one of the video tapes is dust-free, where the others have not been disturbed in months. It contains footage of Michelle Mink in what seems to be a crack den, taking repeated hits off a pipe. (**Data Retrieval** allows a character to hook the copying deck to a laptop monitor for immediate viewing. Otherwise the group will have to wait to get to a machine.)

Stacked in a corner are a number of laptops. The one on the top of the stack has a decal of a tropical fish stuck to its lid. It belonged to Irwin Poling. It requires a password to boot up, which can be circumvented with **Data Retrieval**. Over a dozen messages sent to Garth Marquez's email address appear in the outbox of Poling's mailer program. They reveal that Poling was blackmailing the detective with information gained by unconventional means.

The most interesting emails are as follows:

Dear Detective Marquez -

I know who you are better than you know yourself. At night, I see into your conscience. I see what you do. What haunts you. I can feel what's a real memory and what's a fantasy from the subsconscus mind. The bit where you kill that drug dealer guy with your bare fists. The prostitute — what's her name? Jillian? Jody? — the prostitute you let die, because you were worried about what her pimp knew about you. And how you killed him too. With the hammer, in the bathtub, in the empty house with the gray tile on the bathroom walls. The detail, the intensity of the fear and hate—that's a memory dream. Your memory. It's a crazy new world when not even your dreams are safe from spying, isn't it? Well, don't worry. I don't want much. Not gonna kill the golden goose. Just tax you a little bit. Because let's face it you really are a very bad man, and your friends are all bad too, and you deserve to pay. If not in the next life, then in this one. And if not to God, then to me. If there really was a God, this world wouldn't suck so much, would it? So I spoze I will have to do.

Dear Garthy Baby -

The package you sent in exchange for my continued silence re: the contents of your rancid skull was lamentubly light. The more you get inside me, the more I feel I must charge you. Yet you supply less than what was agreed. Sometimes you dream of a guy name of Frank Flinstone. Well I found out his real name is Frank Williams and he's Internal Affairs Division. Just in case you think your head is the only place I'm capable of looking into.

Just put the rest under my door and then next month its 10% more, OK?

MICHELLE CRACKS
SCENE TYPE: CORE
Confronted with the evidence on the tape, Officer Mink breaks down and confesses that she flushed the evidence in Bibby's drug case at Marquez's behest. The footage dates back to "a bad time in my life" two years ago. Marquez found her in the crack den during a raid but covered up her presence there. Until he came to her this week, she had no idea that the SITF had a camera running inside her chosen smokehouse. Marquez threatened to mail the tape to IAD if she didn't lose the Bibby evidence. Despite his bare-knuckle tactics, she thought she was sticking her neck out because Marquez wanted to protect a confidential informant who'd crossed the line a little. She had no idea that Bibby's freedom was the payoff for a prison hit.

Mink agrees to testify against Marquez in exchange for a suspended sentence. (It goes without saying that she'll be turfed from the force.) Her testimony opens the way for murder conspiracy charges against Marquez and the others. Williams, if consulted, ventures that these charges will likely prove the tip of the iceberg, if they can flip a member of Garth's crew.

SHOWDOWN

SCENE TYPE: CLIMAX

When Officer Mink is arrested, a pal of Collins tips him off. He and the rest of the SITF hunker down at his shooting range out in the boondocks while waiting for an army buddy to arrive and whisk them away in his small plane. If Williams isn't present, **Research** provides the location of Collins' shack.

If the players want it, they can lead the raid to bring them into custody. Or they can choose to let SWAT handle it, opting out of a final action sequence.

When the team arrives at Collins' place, the plane is touching down in a bare field on his property. Marquez and company make a run for the plane, firing their guns to keep arresting officers at bay. The PCs can avoid harm simply by keeping their distance from the plane. If they rush it, they take up to three instances of damage (+2 modifier) when they cross the line of covering fire. A 4-point Athletics spend negates one instance of damage; all characters crossing the line take a minimum of one instance. Creative mutant power use may allow characters to get through the covering fire unharmed, prevent the SITF from firing, or bring the encounter to an end in a different way. Disabling the plane, for example, takes the wind out of Marquez's sails. As corrupt as they are, his crew is only willing to fire directly at other cops (as opposed to laying down suppressive fire) if deadly force is used on them first. If given a chance to surrender when the plane is disabled or covering line breached, they throw down their guns and submit to arrest. Collins' friend, pilot Omer Karsten, carries a pistol but does not participate in the fight.

HARD HELIX

GARTH MARQUEZ

Athletics 6, Fleeing 6, Health 12, Scuffling 9, Shooting 6.

Weapon: H&K MP5 +2, Glock +1

EUSEBIO "U-BOAT" CHAVEZ

Athletics 9, Health 9, Scuffling 12, Shooting 4.

Weapon: H&K MP5 +2, Glock +1

RAY "COLLEY" COLLINS

Athletics 2, Health 4, Scuffling 4, Shooting 8.

Weapon: H&K MP5 +2, Glock +1

DOMINICK ELDER

Athletics 4, Health 2, Scuffling 4, Shooting 4.

Weapon: H&K MP5 +2, Glock +1

SHAWNA SMITH

Athletics 4, Health 2, Scuffling 2, Shooting 6.

Weapon: H&K MP5 +2, Glock +1

WRAP-UP
SCENE TYPE: DENOUEMENT

Under no condition does Marquez cooperate with prosecutors. However, the PCs can flip another team member, ensuring a tighter case against the rest. Your series' regular prosecutor comes on board at this point and tells the group that only the first SITFer who flips gets a deal. The D.A. wants as many of them as possible to see hard jail time. Flipping a team member requires a 2-point Interpersonal spend. Knowing how to approach them may require additional research into their personal lives. The first to flip gets a suspended sentence and maybe even witness protection placement.

A **Negotiation** spend, along with an offer of witness protection to get him away from his gambling debtors, eventually prompts a rueful Ray Collins to offer testimony.

Reassurance soothes Elder's worried conscience, convincing him that only the truth will set him free.

U-Boat cracks under **Intimidation**; beneath his gung-ho exterior is a man terrified of what happens to cops in prison.

A **Cop Talk** spend prompts Smith to roll over, for the sake of her relatives on the force.

Flipping a conspirator is a grace note and is not necessary to successful case completion. See the accompanying tables for sentences with or without witnesses.

With a cooperating witness, more murders are conclusively uncovered, increasing sentences for everyone else.

	WITH WITNESS	WITHOUT
Marquez	Life	20 years
U-Boat	Life	10 years
Smith	20 years	10 years
Collins	10 years	4 years
Elder	8 years	4 years

If a witness flips and the enormity of Marquez's crimes are exposed, the detectives gain the benefit of the doubt from their immediate colleagues. Rank and file uniformed officers may persist in giving them the skunk-eye.

Without a flipped witness, the detectives may continue to get the blue chill from everyone, until they crack some other dramatic case that seems to redeem their credentials as straight-up cops.

CHARACTER QUICK REFERENCE

Ennis Anthony – gangster

Danny Aube – anti-mutant jerk

Sgt Ralph Barbieri - officer in charge of the property department

Marlene Bartholomew - warehouse supervisor

Jeff Bibby – prisoner

Tad Borman – anti-mutant jerk

Travis Brakkee - Assistant warden

Devon Bullock - resourceful but paranoid junkie

Gus Bruner – Irwin Poling's co-worker

De Andre "Sparks" Byrd – gangster

Eusebio "U-Boat" Chavez – SITF member

Ray "Colley" Collins – SITF member

Chloe Dunkin - massage parlor worker

Dominick Elder – SITF member

Tequila Encinas - transvestite prostitute mutant

Frank Flintstone – Garth Marquez's nickname for Frank Williams

Rhino Gomez – gangster

Mike Griffin - lieutenant of Richard Jason

(David Harpe) – football player with mutant strength

Bob Harris – regular at Nets sports bar

Adam Hemphill - chief of detectives

Ray "Little Rex" Henderson – gangster

Nasim Iqbal - Self-pitying cafeteria worker

Richard Wayne Jason - Neutral Parity League youth wing leader

Jimmy the Mope - a shiftless meth-head mutant

Omer Karsten – pilot

Lucille King – Assistant District Attorney

Wolfgang Korn – apartment superintendent

Jonathan Lynch – Hothead mutant activist

Joe Mahlum – anti-mutant jerk

Garth Marquez – head of the SITF

Clarissa Mile - manager of Urban Reef

Officer Michelle Mink – police property clerk

(Edison Mullan) - injured quarterback of the local football team

Vincent Nikula – storage facility owner

Tom Philson - lieutenant of Richard Jason

Irwin Poling – murder victim

Carla Porter – owner/bartender of Nets sports bar

Conrad Priestley - NPL leader

Bridget Renaud aka "Lynette the Lightshow" – regular at Nets sports bar

Oscar Rosario – anti-mutant jerk

Frederick "Fast Freddy" Rossum – regular at Nets sports bar

Dustin Shepherd – anti-mutant jerk

Watch Commander Jonah Smith - uncle to SITF member Shawna Smith.

Shawna Smith – SITF member

Kenneth Westray – barhead

Desiree Whitson – NPL member

Frank Williams – Internal Affairs investigator

Lamar Yancey – drug lord

Ruthie Yi – coffee shop waitress

CELL DIVISION

The HCIU confronts a homegrown terrorist threat from a previously unknown group of mutant supremacists. Can they learn the truth behind the Mutant Revolutionary Front — one that remains shrouded even from its own suicidally indoctrinated followers?

BACKSTORY

Charismatic purported mutant Russ Davenport founded the Mutant Revolutionary Vanguard twelve months ago, building it from a core of suggestible gene-expressives. These including Jeffrey Milan, a self-hating disease-immune mutant, and emotionally lost biotech engineer (and wall crawler) Patricia Gaines.

THE CRIME

Now that he has his followers sufficiently indoctrinated and combat-ready, Davenport strikes quickly, engineering a **Super Siege**: a bold strike against hapless civilians in a heavily trafficked tourist district. (This interrupts an otherwise unrelated comic relief opener, **Lucky Shoes**.)

THE INVESTIGATION

Although the terrorists who participate in this first-wave attack are programmed to kill themselves to evade capture, intervention by the PCs may leave some of them alive. Interviews (or documentary evidence left behind by the dead) reveal a **Chillingly Fanatical** disregard for life. **Background Checks** show similar psychological profiles for all of the MRV killers: young, bright, anchorless men and women who proved ripe for ideological manipulation.

Meanwhile, media coverage of the attack stokes panic, throughout the city and beyond. The arrival of a **Mutant Manifesto** adds urgency to the investigation. The brass encourages a detective to appear on a cable news show **The Big Bulletin**, leading to an ugly explosion of on-air anti-mutant sentiment.

The stakes increase further in **Death On the Tracks**, when, in an echo of the Aum Shin Rikyo subway poisoning, the disease-immune Jeffrey Milan releases a deadly pathogen during rush hour. Analysis of the **Super Pox** traces its origin to a university research lab. In **Container SY-7**, a visit to the lab turns up forensic evidence linking the theft of the virus to wall-crawling student Patricia Gaines. **Trailing Gaines** leads the squad to a conVanguardation with Davenport's remaining terrorists, in **Faces Of Terror**.

THE TWIST

As **Ringleader**, Davenport has insulated himself from his pawns. However, a test on bullets used on his gun range leads the investigators to him—and to his true allegiance, as an anti-mutant activist.

THE CULPRIT

By proving to Davenport's erstwhile allies that he was using them, the investigators get them to roll over on him, closing the case.

SCENES

LUCKY SHOES

SCENE TYPE: FALSE OPENING / COMIC RELIEF

As the case opens, the investigators are embroiled in another investigation—one of comically absurd proportions. Play this as the sort of comic interrogation used as a staple element of shows like *NYPD Blue*.

Cut back and forth between interviews between the case's three central figures:

- the complainant, a demanding middle-aged lady named Bonnie Kreger.

- her son, Gerry Kreger, a skinny, evasive young man who pings **Bullshit Detector** like crazy and shows the bruises and contusions of a recent beatdown.

- Romeo "the Mule" Olivieri, a mob-tied[1] restaurant owner who shrugs and makes ridiculous excuses while picking bits of lint from his ill-fitting Armani suit jacket.

Fill the players in on what has happened prior to the scene opening. Bonnie came in to complain that her son was assaulted. He told her that the owner of Olivieri's Steak House had him beaten up for looking at the man's girlfriend. Bonnie wants Olivieri charged with assault. She doesn't believe the girlfriend story; she thinks her son is the victim of an anti-mutant hate crime. Bonnie claims that her son is able to project his thoughts, even though he is in the closet and denies his true superheroic potential.

Gerry denies saying any such thing to his mother. "Lookit me. Do you think a guy like that has anything to worry about, me looking at his woman?" He says he tripped and fell near the restaurant, after having a few too many. **Streetwise** suggests that Gerry is too scared to tell the real story. He also furiously denies being a mutant.

"The Mule", whose rap sheet (**Research**) shows him to have a long history of gambling-related offenses, repeats Gerry's story—suspiciously repeating many of the same words and phrases, as if they've agreed on an account to police. Naturally, this too tweaks detectives' **Bullshit Detector**s.

After establishing the situation, allow the PCs to quickly drill down to the truth, after facing only amusingly transparent denials.

Gerry is a mutant, which led to his beating, but not out of prejudice. Romeo runs an illicit casino in a warehouse near his restaurant. Gerry possesses the Technopathy power, and used it to predict when Romeo's slots would pay off. After pulling this trick one time too many, Romeo confronted him. Gerry claimed to have won only because he was wearing his lucky shoes. This show of disrespect led to his ejection from the establishment—with additional punching and kicking to drive home the point. As he tells the story, Gerry repeats his feeble claim that he won on account of his shoes. Shown a Quade Diagram, and the proximity of Telepathy (which his mother says he has) and Technopathy, Gerry cops to the truth. He still, however, refuses to press charges against The Mule, who he acknowledges was entirely justified in having him roughed up.

Before the squad can get any further in pressing a case against The Mule, the lieutenant bursts in and tells them their priorities have suddenly changed—there's a crisis in progress.

SUPER SIEGE
SCENE TYPE: OPENING / ACTION

This scene takes place at your chosen city's main cultural district or installation. Many major cities cluster cultural institutions together on a reclaimed waterfront; this scene might happen there. It has to be a place where large numbers of local residents and tourists gather. Pick a location where people normally feel safe and secure. It has been targeted for precisely that reason—a strike there will seem doubly shocking than one in an anonymous or sketchy location.

Patrol dispatches from the scene, as passed along by the squad's lieutenant, inform them that a group of masked mutant attackers have wandered into a milling crowd and opened fire with their deadly powers.

When the squad arrives, the MRV terror team has hunkered down behind a makeshift barricade of crumpled SWAT vehicles. These were taken and smashed into place by an attacker named Josie Pearl. Josie herself has not taken refuge behind the shattered police vans. She crouches behind a large air vent on the roof of a nearby building, waiting to swoop down opportunistically on any attackers. PCs spot her on a Difficulty 4 Surveillance test.

SWAT teams have cordoned off a perimeter. Uniformed officers keep reporters and heedless rubberneckers at bay. Seven bodies lie sprawled on the ground around the shield of vans. Three are SWAT officers, another a patrolman. Also dead on the spot are two young adult males and an elderly woman. Further away, paramedic crews load other victims into ambulances. Teams from the medical examiner's officers lay out over a dozen bodies. Body bags have been requisitioned and

---
[1] If you haven't yet run **The Vanishers**, you can use this as an opportunity to lay pipe for that scenario, by specifying that Olivieri's ties are to the Vetroni crime family.

HARD HELIX

are on their way from the city's nearest emergency management depot. T-shirts from a nearby vendor's stand cover the faces of the slain.

The SWAT commander has already commandeered news and civilian video footage of the initial assault. He offers to show it to the squad before they make their move. They can view it on a monitor in his trailer-like mobile command post. He is Lieutenant Ken Swailes, who they may remember from the hostage sequence that opens Mutant City Blues' sample scenario, "Food Chain." Swailes, a lanky, long-faced man, mops his perpetually sweating brow with a damp handkerchief.

The footage shows a tightly packed but happy crowd suddenly fly into a panic. The handheld shots blur wildly as panicked camera holders flee. Masked figures lurch into view. All of them wear black coveralls, work boots, and black masks. Shaded goggles protect their eyes, lending them an implacably bug-like appearance. One of the figures points at a vacationing couple and causes their flesh to blacken and fall from their bones.

Anamorphology identifies this power as Radiation Projection.

Another summons swarming insects to panic the crowd, bringing about a fatal stampede. A third freezes his victims with an ice blast.

The only woman terrorist captured on camera flies above the crowd, killing with beams of flesh-cooking energy. **Anamorphology** pegs this as Heat Blast.

Swailes says there's a fifth perpetrator not seen on any of the footage, and that she may have water powers.

Although this is an act of political violence, the terrorists do not communicate with the PCs, or anyone else. Their ideology will be explained later, perhaps after their deaths, with the release of a manifesto. All are fanatically willing to die. Except for Chee, all have been issued cyanide pills, which they will use if their capture seems imminent. Telescopic Vision or Read Minds may allow characters to spot the attempt to take these pills before they are swallowed. Chee, who is immune to toxins, will instead attempt to guarantee suicide-by-cop, by getting himself killed during arrest. Before they die, the terrorists want to kill as many police officers as possible. When the squad comes after them, they fight without relent. Considering themselves dead already, they are more interested in ensuring indelibly memorable news footage than fighting to maximum defensive advantage. For example, Ferdinand Licata might send a swarm of birds against an enemy rather than simply opening fire with his pistol.

The terrorists have used some of their powers already. The game statistics given below reflect their pools when the squad arrives on the scene. If they unexpectedly reappear in your series at a later date, you may want to increase their pools to reflect their fully refreshed states.

JAYSON "HIROSHIMA" CHEE

A slightly stocky third generation Chinese-American in his late twenties.

Athletics 4, Fleeing 4, Health 12, Scuffling 4, Shooting 8

Powers: Radiation Immunity 8, Radiation Projection 13, Toxin Immunity (Ingested) 4

Weapon: assault rifle +1

MARY "H2O" DELOZIER

Thin, pale, blond-haired woman in her early thirties. She keeps her hair in a lank, mousy mess.

Athletics 2, Fleeing 2, Health 8, Scuffling 2, Shooting 3

Powers: Toxin Immunity (Inhaled) 6, Water Blast 11, Water Manipulation 6

Weapon: automatic pistol 0

FERDINAND "ICEWING" LICATA

Tall, goateed man with dark, piercing eyes in his mid twenties.

Athletics 8, Health 10, Scuffling 4, Shooting 2

Powers: Command Birds 12, Ice Blast 12, Reduce Temperature 8

Weapon: automatic pistol 0

BILLY "BLOOD BUG" MORAN

Freckled, red-faced, blond man in his early twenties.

Athletics 6, Health 2, Scuffling 3, Shooting 9

Powers: Blood Spray 15, Command Insects 11, Induce Fear 11

Weapon: automatic pistol 0

JOSIE "TUNGUSKA" PEARL

Willowy, high-cheekboned young woman of mixed African American and native heritage.

Athletics 12, Fleeing 12, Health 6, Scuffling 8

Powers: Flight 8, Heat Blast 10, Regeneration 10, Strength 6

CHILLINGLY FANATICAL
SCENE TYPE: ALTERNATE

If the PCs are lucky or clever, they may be able to capture one or more of the terrorists alive. Jayson Chee, unable to kill himself with cyanide pills, is the most likely survivor.

None of the attackers are cooperative witnesses. They'll talk about their ideology with glassy-eyed fervor, but refuse to identify themselves by their "human names" or discuss their ordinary lives. Instead, they answer only to their super code names.

They all provide roughly the same information, filtered through their individual personality quirks:

Jayson "Hiroshima" Chee affects a perpetual scowl to harden his baby-faced features.

HARD HELIX

Mary "H2O" Delozier is passive-aggressively confrontational. She sulks, as if the detectives have wronged her, ought to be apologizing for it, and should also understand what they've done to offend her without being told.

Ferdinand "Icewing" Licata treats even the slightest pressure from a male interrogator as a challenge to his macho authority. Though raised in the United States, a faint hint of accent remains from his southern Italian childhood.

Billy "Blood Bug" Moran underlines his pugnacious attitude with copious profanity. Unlike the others, who come from privileged backgrounds, Moran is a two-fisted child of the streets. His attachment to the MRV is as a cure for his feelings of powerlessness.

Josie "Tunguska" Pearl spews hateful, apocalyptic rhetoric with the verbal facility of a radicalized Humanities lecturer.

- They launched their attacks on behalf of the Mutant Revolutionary Vanguard.

- Unlike the species traitors of the HIA and the childish dilettantes of the Genetic Action Front, the Mutant Revolutionary Vanguard is not content to merely flirt with its agenda.

- The revolution they seek is real, and literal. Thus the real weapons of revolution, including terror, must be utilized without qualm or hesitation.

- Mutants represent only 1% of the world's population. According to the inexorable laws of political power, they must either become the exploiters, or be exploited themselves.

- Humans are weak-minded and lazy. Throughout history, the masses have been willingly acquiesced in their own domination, surrendering control to numerically tiny ruling classes.

- The Mutant Revolutionary Vanguard will make the gene expressive the global ruling class of the 21st century. Their actions will terrify humankind, prompting cowardly and ignorant reprisals against mutantkind. Forced to choose sides, those mutants who now foolishly believe themselves part of the human race will, in the final analysis, elect to join this new ruling class.

- Global civil war between norms and gene-expressives is inevitable outcome with or without the MRV. They merely accelerate its timing, so that it occurs before mutants have been slowly weakened by decades of suppression and media-sponsored self-loathing.

- MRV includes suicidal tactics in its arsenal to show the weak and easily cowed human populace the fiery righteousness of mutant determination.

- As mutant police officers, the PCs are quislings of the worst and most ignorant sort. For the moment they act as tame lapdogs for the norms. Yet one day the irresistible tides of history will sweep them into allegiance with their true genetic kin. Then they will reap the benefits of the revolution they now blindly impede.

Influence Detection shows that none of them have been affected by mind-altering powers.

Forensic Psychology likens their behavior to fanatics or cult members. They have clearly been subjected to intensive indoctrination, but probably entered into the group willingly. Each displays telltale personality traits associated with extreme radicalism. Low empathy and feelings of alienation from society couple with a fierce desire for certitude and an aversion to shades of gray. They also show symptoms of Post-Mutation Adjustment Disorder (PMAD), a personality disorder that arises when a person becomes gene-expressive and is unable to smoothly assimilate this new development into his or her sense of identity.

BACKGROUND CHECKS
SCENE TYPE: ALTERNATE

The squad is more likely to learn about the attackers from legwork conducted after their deaths. Even if they are alive, their relatives will tell more about them than they will about themselves.

None carry identification. The pockets of their coveralls are largely empty, except for spare ammo clips and a distinctively odd assortment of small items: a Hello Kitty cellphone charm (Chee), a packet of Malaysian mints (Delozier), a lighter bearing an image of rock performer Carlos Santana (Licata), a thumb drive containing video files of several episodes of the game show *Triple Dare* (Moran) and a fake jade figurine of a dragon (Pearl.)

Research yields fingerprint hits for Billy Moran and Mary Delozier. Moran is in the system for a series of misdemeanor arrests, including vandalism and assault. Delozier worked as a civilian employee of the military, performing basic clerical work.

Any of the attackers other than Moran is quickly identified by family members if images of their faces are released to the media.

- Jayson Chee's parents, Simon and Melba Chee, are horrified and humiliated by news of his terror links. He cut himself off from them sixteen months ago, after years of failed treatment for depression. His mental illness coincided, at the age of twelve, with his manifestation of mutant powers. Simon thinks that the two events were unrelated, while Melba blames the mutant powers for the onset of her son's depression. Simon co-owns a very successful real estate development firm. A look at Jayson's room, stuffed to the gills with the latest electronic toys and expensive collectibles, suggests that the Chees spared no material expense in trying to please their troubled son.

JAYSON AND ARTICLE 18

Bureaucracy turns up no Article 18 filing for Jayson Chee. His parents are shocked to learn that their son possessed Article 18 powers. They knew that he had Toxin Immunity, discovered when he drank a pint of weedkiller on a dare, to no ill effect. He also led them to believe he had Kinetic Energy Dispersal. The Chees assure the detectives that they would have insisted on their son properly registering his power, if only they had known about it.

- Mary Delozier is identified by her mother, Catherine Semple. She traces her daughter's disaffection to her remarriage when Mary was 13. Over the past year Mary has been forwarding politically inflammatory mutant rights emails to her mother. Semple never inquired about Delozier's new circle of friends. **Forensic Psychology** suggests that Catherine wanted to kibosh discussion of the entire topic. Mrs. Semple shyly admits to mutant powers of her own, but says that she never uses them, because she's afraid of getting asthma. **Anamorphology** (or a glance at the Quade Diagram) suggest that her powers are Deplete Oxygen and Wind Control. **Reassurance** is needed to get her to confirm this.

- Ferdinand Licata's father Eugenio is a famed automotive engineer. **Trivia** names him as designer of the popular Zipster mid-priced sports car. He comes off as a driven workaholic who lost track of his son while pursuing his high-pressure career. Eugenio says he hates politics of all kinds and discouraged his son from involvement in mutant rights activities. He thought that Ferdinand belonged to the Genetic Action Front, which was bad enough. Eugenio seems ready to disown his son—posthumously, if Ferdinand was killed during "Super Siege."

- Moran's relatives do not come forward. The fingerprint hit, plus **Research**, brings detectives to the door of his next of kin, his grizzled, booze-soaked uncle Teddy Moran. His mother disappeared when he was sixteen; his father, a suspect in her apparent murder, died while imprisoned on an unrelated charge three years later. Teddy says that Billy always was gullible, but joining a gang that not only doesn't pay but also wants you to kill yourself is the height of stupid. Although Moran regards his nephew's upbringing as normal, his account nonetheless paints a picture of neglect and abuse.

- Josie Pearl's parents, Joseph Pearl and Marie White Cloud, are both academics at the city's most prestigious university. Both have a history of political radicalism but were upset to see their very bright daughter flirt with the violent tactics they turned their backs on as young activists in the mid 1980s. She remained in touch with them even as the MRV tightened its grip on her. At one point, she promised to arrange a meeting between her parents

HARD HELIX

and her cell leader, who she referred to by the codename Keratin. To Josie's apparent dismay, Keratin called off the meeting. Shortly thereafter they saw her in person for the last time, about three months ago. (**Chemistry**: keratin is the fibrous protein used by the body to create structures arising from the skin, like hair and fingernails.)

MUTANT MANIFESTO
SCENE TYPE: ANTAGONIST REACTION

Punctuate the investigation scenes with periodic references to the alarmed, mournful media coverage of the attack, which is quickly termed the Waterfront Massacre. (Substitute a more appropriate local name for the site of the killings if you prefer.) Just as the media runs out of new news to report about the siege, the MRV ramps up public anxiety by releasing the following manifesto via email to major print and broadcast outlets. It arrives as a PDF file bearing the crudely designed logo of the Mutant Revolutionary Vanguard as a watermark beneath the text.

```
Mutant Revolutionary Front
Takes Responsibility For
Waterfront Massacre

The Mutant Revolutionary Front declares it-
self the instrument of the so-called Water-
front Massacre. More attacks will follow.

We carry out violence against humankind as a
necessary preemptive strike against its past
and future violence against us. Everywhere
the gene expressive have proclaimed their
status as an emergent species, they have
been mocked, savaged, and oppressed.

The Mutant Revolutionary Front, steeped in
historical dialectic, sees that the arrival
of a new sapient species presages inevitable
conflict with the old. It is only a matter of
time before the superseded begin a program
of genocidal cleansing aimed at scrubbing
our kind from the face of the planet. Na-
turally, we will and must survive. To this
end we spur the gene expressive community to
seize the levers of world power, before we
are too weakened to strike.

The Mutant Revolutionary Vanguard is ready
to sacrifice the lives of its best and bra-
vest to achieve ultimate victory. Lacking
numbers, determination must be our adaptive
trait. We must demonstrate the ferocity of
wolves, or be whipped like dogs. An army of
martyrs stands ready to do battle. In a war
between species, there are no bystanders, no
innocents. All targets are legitimate.

It is not our expectation that our victory
in the amoral Darwinian struggle to come
will be an easy one. Our demand is nothing
less than worldwide global dominance. We do
not expect that this will be granted without
further bloodshed.

So further bloodshed it will be.

To our gene expressive brethren, we say:
Brace yourselves for worldwide genetic war-
fare. Be prepared to defend yourself to the
death against reprisal attacks, whether they
come from your mothers, your fathers, your
brothers, your children. There are only two
sides in this war. Them and us. In your al-
tered bones, you know this.

Until we rule the world, it is kill or be
killed.
```

Data Retrieval shows that the message was sent via an offshore anonymizer service, which will be impossible to track. Anyone with a middling degree of web savvy could have pulled this off.

To prove that the communique is genuine, the accompanying email lists the oddball items found in each terrorist's pocket. (If the detectives have released this information to the press, they'll now realize to their chagrin that they've muddied the identification.)

The arrival of the manifesto triggers bureaucratic alarm bells within the department. Now that the incident has been confirmed as a terrorist incident, the federal authorities want to take over the case. Like any police organization, the department wants to dig in and protect its turf. The lieutenant comes to the squad and demands an update that he can take to the brass, who in turn can reassure the mayor and district attorney.

THE BIG BULLETIN
SCENE TYPE: DRAMA

As political pressure to reassure the public mounts, word comes down from on high that one or two of the most media-ready PCs should appear live on the national cable show *The Big Bulletin*, to field questions from the host, Jim Hutchins.

Trivia shows that Hutchins is a typical cable blowhard. He's an iconoclastic right winger with predictable law and order views—and thus a likely provider of the softball questions that will make the force look good.

Before the broadcast, the lieutenant briefs the PCs who will be appearing on the show.

- Their first priority is to calm the public. The force especially wants to avoid the sorts of vigilante actions against mutants that might escalate fears of the MRV's predicted war between norms and chromes coming to pass.

- Next, they're to encourage the public to come forward with tips that could lead to the rest of the terror cell.

- Finally, they're to convey the impression that the local force has the case well in hand. It doesn't need to be turned over to the feds.

- While doing this, they're to provide as little information as possible regarding the investigation. As they would with any journalist, they can expect Hutchins to keep probing for a scoop.

Hutchins, a thick-necked former pro football player turned hard-edged pundit, begins the interview as expected—repeatedly pressing the PCs to provide more information. When that fails, he calls on them to speculate as to the size, history, and composition of the Mutant Revolutionary Front.

Once this phase of the interview stalls, he turns on them, aggressively demanding that they justify the force's decision to keep mutant cops on the case. Isn't this a conflict of interest? Hutchins doesn't come right out and make the accusation himself, but implies that unnamed others might worry that gene expressive police officers might secretly sympathize with the MRV. Shouldn't they recuse themselves from the case?

Press the players' buttons as obnoxiously as you can while remaining within the realistic bounds of what a hot-button TV personality might say on the air. The scene underlines the story's stakes by testing the players' ability to remain politic under a blistering verbal barrage.

If they stay on message, they win approval from the lieutenant. Should they lose their cool, he gives them a chewing out upon their return to HQ. The mayor's office saw the interview, and is now considering turning the case over to the feds. This, needless to say, would be a huge blow to the credibility of the entire unit.

TURF WARS

If you feel yourself in need of an additional drama sub-plot, insert nosy federal liaison officers into the mix. As in any procedural show, investigators who are not the main characters appear in the story to add complicating factors. These feds are arrogant boneheads who fixate on a mistaken theory of the case. They convince themselves that the MRV is a front for a foreign threat, aggressively challenging the PCs when their evidence leads elsewhere. Special Agent Allen Sanford is a jowly bulldog of a man who injects testosterone-fueled competitiveness into the smallest of interactions.
Special Agent Gloria Stefaniuk seeks the upper hand by adopting the classic ice maiden role. Fortified by coldly glamorous hair and makeup, she speaks with brittle, contemptuous precision.
Neither of them make any effort to hide their lack of confidence in local cops. After "The Big Bulletin", they parrot public concerns that enhanced detectives lack the distance to properly pursue the case.
A romantic sub-plot might be inserted here, with one of the feds given a vulnerable side, making him or her attractive to the PC most amenable to such a storyline.

Special Agent Allen Sanford
Athletics 3, Health 2, Scuffling 6, Shooting 8.
Weapon: 0 (Glock)

Special Agent Gloria Stefaniuk
Athletics 2, Health 3, Scuffling 4, Shooting 10.
Weapon: 0 (Glock)

HARD HELIX

DEATH ON THE TRACKS

SCENE TYPE: ANTAGONIST REACTION

Soon after the (possibly disastrous) TV appearance, the detective appearing on the Hutchins show receives a cell phone call. A male voice, electronically altered, coolly informs them that they have chosen the wrong side in the civil war between the species, and are destined for the ash heap of history. Before the PC can engage him in debate, he names a major subway station, and says, "Two minutes."

(If your chosen mutant city lacks an underground rail system, select another suitable enclosed space for this sequence. Davenport picks the location to maximize public panic. He wants a spot many people frequently travel to, so that they can readily imagine themselves there at the time of the attack.)

Ninety-seven seconds after Davenport hangs up, Jeffrey Milan, already in position in a subway car roaring into the station, unscrews the top of what looks to be a thermal coffee container and leaves it under his seat. Within seconds, riders inside the half-full car are stricken by an array of horrifying symptoms. Lesions open up and bleed under the skin, blackening it. The whites of victims' eyes redden. Blood fills the lungs, leading to collapse and asphyxiation. Milan, immune to disease, strides calmly out of the subway car as the invisible viral cloud billows out through its doors onto the platform. There dozens of other passengers are stricken. Although terrifyingly virulent, the viral cloud disperses quickly. Subway patrons more than 300 meters from the infected car suffer a spotting of lesions and reddening of the eyes, but do not collapse or drown in their own blood. Four of these less affected victims nonetheless suffer fatal heart attacks or strokes, rendered vulnerable by preexisting medical conditions.

Squad members may be first on the scene but are presumably unable to arrive quickly enough to intercept Milan. The scene is impossible to control, as panicked patrons lurch for the exits. If the squad are the first responders to arrive on the scene, they may find creative ways to use their super powers to calm the crowd or to prevent bystanders from being trampled.

Forensic Anthropology warns that prudent practice requires the team to cordon off the station and wait for Hazmat teams to arrive from the Center For Disease Control (or a like emergency service.) If the team goes in anyway, danger of infection has already been significantly reduced. Characters with Disease Immunity are unaffected. Anyone else entering the hot zone during the first hour of the mop-up makes a Difficulty 4 Health roll to avoid minor infection from the super pox. Failed characters experience reddened eyes and uneven patches spots of bruised, blackened skin. For the duration of the case, they lose an additional 2 Health each time they suffer an instance of damage.

When the disease control team arrives, a dispute over priorities arises. The scrubbers want to treat it as a possible vector of an unknown and dangerous contagion. If the detectives don't fight to preserve it as a crime scene, the feds will. After a period of wrangling and calls to superiors word comes down from the highest authorities that disease control is a higher priority than evidence preservation.

Hazmat suits are made available for the squad to quickly survey and photograph the scene before the scrubbing takes place. Dozens of appallingly distressed corpses lie strewn through the subway car and platform. Sight of the unscrubbed scene counts as a crisis which may exacerbate any of the following Stability-based defects: Addictive Personality, Attention Deficit Disorder, Depression, Dissociation, Messiah Complex, Panic Disorder, or Schizophrenia.

(core) If they insist on being present at the scene, a detective with **Evidence Collection** spots the coffee container going into a quarantined bin for destruction.

With some victims lingering in hospital, the death toll from the attack continues to mount over a period of days. The immediate toll is 36, going up to 38 the next day, 39 the day after that, until it finally settles at 41 two days later.

A security camera clearly points at the door to the infected car. The footage reveals the chain of events described above. A young, clean-cut man steps calmly through the car's doors, unaffected by the fast-spreading disease as passengers are stricken all around him. Clad in a wind breaker, polo shirt, dress slacks and suede loafers, the suspect seems to pause for an instant to smirk up into the camera lens. Then he bobs out of sight. The players will probably get this one without assistance: if necessary, **Anamorphology** reminds them that Disease Immunity is a mutant power.

Electronic Surveillance spots, in a freeze-frame of his smirk, signs that Milan has fangs.

TRACING THE CALL
SCENE TYPE: ALTERNATE

Electronic Surveillance reveals that that the phone Davenport uses to place the call is a mobile number registered to Jayson Chee.

On a 1-point **Electronic Surveillance** spend, the detective accesses the cellular network to pinpoint the phone's current location. When it pops up, it is rapidly moving, as if its user is in a vehicle. The vehicle is headed toward a major sports stadium. When patrol cars are scrambled to intercept the vehicle, it turns out to be a taxi. Someone has taken the phone and wedged it into the passenger seat cushion. The phone is wrapped in a copy of the MRV manifesto.

Data Retrieval on the phone's content concludes that Chee used it with a careful eye to operational security. Its address book and calling history contain only a few red flag numbers, in addition to those for his family and innocuous businesses, such as a pizza delivery joint. The only numbers that pop out are for four phones purchased around the same time as this one, each entered under the code name of a dead or captured colleague: Blood Bug, H20, Tunguska, and Icewing. **Forensic Accounting** turns up billing records affirming that Chee purchased the phone only a few weeks before the Waterfront Massacre.

The officer receiving the call may wonder how the MRV got the number for his work mobile. Finding out takes a half day's worth of **Research** legwork, which can be cut to an hour with a 2-point spend. The detective gave his number to the producers of the Hutchins show. One of Hutchins assistants gave the number to a woman who called posing as a booker for another cable news show. The assistant is Giselle Clauson, a pretty and now incredibly nervous young woman scarcely out of journalism school. A 1-point **Reassurance** spend is required to get her to talk immediately; otherwise she waits to hire a lawyer, which delays the inquiry by a couple of days. When she does cooperate, she describes the voice she heard as young, with a hint of a disguised southern accent. (If your mutant city is in the south, pick another regional accent that would stand out as unusual, and that a career-minded person might make an effort to soften.)

Clauson's caller was Patricia Gaines, acting under Davenport's instructions.

HUNTING MILAN
SCENE TYPE: ALTERNATE

If the team releases Milan's image, either as a still or in video clip form, to the media, they're deluged with phone calls about him. As always in a high profile case like this, the crazy and unfounded tips outnumber the useful ones by a huge margin. A **Research** spend is necessary to promptly sift the legitimate tips from the nonsense: 2 points correctly identifies Milan within 24 hours, 1 point the next day. On the third day, information sifts out without a spend.

The first tipster they come across is 23-year old mechanical engineering student Rocky Riele, who remembers the man on the video as former classmate Jeffrey Milan. Riele, a hybrid of hipster and nerd, wears an odd T-Shirt which **Trivia** identifies as a reference to this week's Internet in-joke. He explains that he briefly allowed the socially maladroit Milan into his study group. Rocky recalls Milan as a quietly argumentative, passive-aggressive fellow who flitted quickly between new interests and hobbies. These included ambient music, cold war memorabilia, and the online video game Global Threat. At one point Milan claimed to have invented a foolproof card-counting scheme and tried to recruit Riele for a trip to Vegas to win at blackjack. Rocky told Jeffery to take a hike after his awkward attempts to hit on the women in the group became intolerable. Although Milan rarely talked about his past, he did allude to having been raised in the foster care system.

Other witnesses come forward, confirming the identification while providing little additional information:

- The gum-chewing, overly made-up Bernice Hollings was Milan's foster mother for six months when he was sixteen. She describes him as a "back-talking snot" and "exactly the kind of little bastard you'd expect to do this kind of thing." Hollings' main interest is in whatever reward money she can squeeze out of the system.

HARD HELIX

- An athletic and blandly good-looking former roommate, Dan Haskin, describes Milan as a selfish guy who ate food he didn't pay for and never did the dishes. Haskin admits that he got back at him by pinning articles about SEDS on Milan's door. For some reason, Milan was totally freaked out that he might be a SEDS carrier.

- Genetic Action Front leader Sharon Bryson (*Mutant City Blues*, p. 154) reluctantly comes forward to admit that Milan was briefly a member, about a year and a half ago. He was very clingy and wanted to be the center of attention at all times. (**Forensic Psychology** suggests that Bryson has room in her life for only one narcissistic attention-seeker—herself.) After she rebuffed his offer to build an expensive IT setup for the group, he grew sulky and accused them of not being "real" enough.

None of these background witnesses has any clue to Milan's current whereabouts.

SUPER POX
SCENE TYPE: CORE

(core) **Chemistry** finds a pure sample of the pathogen inside the coffee container. The detective identifies unique manufactured genetic markers in the virus. Checking the marker's entry in Homeland Security bio-threat database, the investigator discovers its origin. It was genetically engineered at the biotech research lab of the city's top science university.

The head of the biotech department, Dr. Trina Ward, cooperates readily with the investigation. She's alarmed that the incident might permanently sully the university's reputation. Ward arranges a meeting for detectives with Dr. David Sussman, the researcher who registered the telltale genetic marker.

The energetic, hyper-verbal Sussman assures the detectives that his engineered retrovirus was in no way a pathogen. He has been working for years on a virus as a delivery system for tumor-killing cells. He calls this the USR, or universal switch receptor. A successful USR holds out the potential for cancer treatments that cure without the collateral damage wreaked on the body by chemo and radiation therapy. Though appalled by the subway deaths, his main priority is to ensure that his research, which could save untold lives, is not derailed by association with terrorism. **Chemistry** suggests that Sussman is downplaying a damaging fact about his research—that the very adaptability of his virus also makes it an ideal delivery system for bio-warfare pathogens. With access to a sample of the USR, even a grad student can take an existing bacterium or virus and turn it into a deadly threat.

If asked, Sussman explains that the USR is designed to break down quickly when exposed to a living immune system, and to render its payload non-communicable. Without these components, the subway attack could have taken out half the city. (**Chemistry** suggests that Sussman is again downplaying. Without this kill-switch, the pathogen could have touched off a global pandemic[2].)

In a clumsy attempt to show his affinity to mutants, Sussman explains that the USR was isolated from cells found in latent mutants. It is a by-product of the Sudden Mutation Event.

In any event, he argues that his lab must have been the victim of cyber-espionage. The terrorists must have broken into his hard drive and appropriated the method of synthesis for USR. Lab security is too tight to allow anyone to have taken actual samples. His students, who he trusts implicitly, are nonetheless subjected to routine search to prevent any of the USR from being removed from the lab.

CONTAINER SY-7
SCENE TYPE: CORE

An expert in **Electronic Surveillance** can see that security in the lab itself is indeed state of the art. USR samples are stored in metal cannisters in a highly secured room.

However, **Evidence Collection** quickly turns up a cannister that is not like the others. Its sealing ring is cracked, suggesting that it the cannister is older than the others. It is labeled SY-7.

Chemistry confirms that the sample in SY-7 is not USR, but an inert liquid.

Document Analysis dates the glue on the back of the label on this cannister and shows that it's a different brand, and was placed on the container months later than the labels on the legit items.

---

[2] If the players seem interested and pacing allows it, you may wish to insert a sub-plot concerning the squad's efforts to shut down Sussman's heedless research practices.

(The implication of this evidence: Gaines took another, older container, placed a fake label on it, and substituted it for the real one.)

Evidence Collection finds signs of tampering on the room's window. The room is on the ninth floor of the building, with no easy access from neighboring rooms. If the detectives search the exterior wall for fibers, **Evidence Collection** yields a number of setules—the hairs left behind by a user of the Wall Crawling power. (See *Mutant City Blues*, p. 72.)

(core) **Fingerprinting** finds a prints on the metal window sill. When checked in the forensics lab, one set includes the distinctive striations found in the prints of wall crawlers. Everyone who works in Sussman's lab is fingerprinted as a security measure. These prints correspond to one of his former graduate students, Patricia Gaines.

Dr. Sussman discusses Gaines in glowing terms, until he realizes she's a suspect in the case. He then backpedals furiously, minimizing his connection with her. Sussman is startled to learn that his former lab assistant is a possible terrorist—and nearly as taken aback to hear that she was a secret mutant. Momentarily forgetting who he's talking to, he assures the detectives that he took specific care to screen out mutant candidates. Sussman has the following to say about Gaines:

- She was among his most diligent lab workers. Patricia could always be counted on to do the unglamorous scutwork that really makes a lab run.

- She was a composed, undemonstrative person who kept her complaints and problems to herself.

- Sussman would have happily kept her on, if she'd wanted to continue.

- He never offered her a teaching opportunity, because he didn't want to take her concentration away from their important research work.

- She told him she'd left because she'd found a position at another university, one that would let her teach. He tried to talk her out of it, to no avail.

One of Patricia's former colleagues can shed more light on her personal life. Soft-spoken lab technician Madhura Rawal describes her as:

- extremely driven, but lonely and unsure of herself.

- She grew up in the south, but worked hard to discard her once-thick accent. (This clue suggests that she was the unknown person who got the detective's cell phone number from Jim Hutchins' assistant; see "Tracing the Call", p. 72)

- Patricia never spoke of her romantic life. Just before she left the lab, Madhura spotted her on campus in the company of a tall, broad shouldered man with salt and pepper hair. The man loomed over Patricia in a possessive way, making Madhura think that he might have been a boyfriend. (This is Russ Davenport.)

- When she asked her about him, Patricia seemed stricken and changed the subject. Madhura assumed from this that the man was married.

Sussman still has Gaines' address.

TRAILING GAINES

SCENE TYPE: CORE

If the detectives have already captured and interrogated members of the MRV from the Waterfront Massacre, they may already realize that Gaines is unlikely to crack if arrested now. Otherwise, a character with **Forensic Psychology** reminds the group that highly indoctrinated terrorists don't easily roll on their confederates. They're likelier to find them by physically trailing her.

Tracking her to the hideout of the terror cell requires the team to stake out her duplex in a quiet residential neighborhood.

The following steps inject interest and suspense into the pursuit sequence. Use them as is, or improvise equivalent moments in response to player choices.

Streetwise allows the team to set up a series of vehicles which can park in the area unnoticed.

HARD HELIX

The terror attacks have everyone on edge. Yvette Boykins, an elderly neighbor on the lookout for evildoers, spots the detectives while on self-appointed stakeout duty and trundles down to confront them. She's sure that the squad members are planning to bomb her neighborhood. As she comes down to raise a fuss, Gaines leaves her apartment. **Cop Talk** calms Yvette down without drawing Gaines' attention.

(If they fail to defuse the Boykins distraction, require a Difficulty 4 Surveillance test to unobtrusively catch up with her. Should this fail, allow Gaines to lead them to the "Faces Of Terror" sequence on a subsequent occasion.)

Gaines heads to her garage and drives off in an anonymous-looking subcompact car. Once she's moving, **Electronic Surveillance**, perhaps in conjunction with police helicopters, allows the detectives to follow her to the outskirts of town. She drives through an industrial park to a tract of undeveloped land. With a nonchalant air suggesting she has done this many times, Gaines gets out of the vehicle to open a padlocked gate. Then she drives through, parks again, clicks the padlock shut, gets back in the car, and drives along an unpaved road running through a wooded area.

FACES OF TERROR
SCENE TYPE: CORE (ACTION)

A wireless Internet search pulls up a satellite map of the multi-acre property. The wooded, hilly area visible from the roadway surrounds what appears to be a derelict gravel quarry. A few small buildings are found on the quarry floor. **Data Retrieval** allows a laptop-equipped character to enhance the computer image to find a pair of newer-looking outbuildings. These are situated in a clearing about half a mile from the quarry. The road Gaines drove onto leads toward them.

Research reveals that the property's current owner is the municipal government. It has been confiscated for non-payment of back taxes. **Law** suggests that this allows the detectives to enter without a warrant. Gaines, and anyone present on the property, is trespassing, and does not enjoy privacy protections against police search or seizure.

The padlock on the gate does not pose a significant obstacle. Bolt cutters, or use of the Strength power, easily dismantles the fence. If the detectives want to enter covertly, without leaving signs of their presence, they can hop the fence, leaving their vehicles on the side of the road. Say yes to clever alternate solutions proposed by the players.

A Difficulty 4 Infiltration test allows detectives to creep up through the wooded area surrounding the newer buildings. This test is piggybacked if attempted by multiple characters. There they spot three additional vehicles.

Alternately, the detectives can call for police helicopters to overfly the area, and get a report on the number of vehicles. However, this trips the conspirators' sense of justified paranoia, causing them to immediately flee.

The conspirators also flee if the detectives make a non-stealthy approach.

However they come near, the detectives note a strong wind blowing up as the takedown beckons.

As Gaines arrives, her co-conspirators occupy the larger of the two structures. If the detectives are close enough to keep tabs on her, they see her entering.

Both structures are prefabricated buildings, their walls made of pressed and painted sheet metal. (**Architecture** shows that they have been hastily constructed and are clearly not up to code.) The main building is the MRV headquarters. The second is a shack-like enclosure, its door secured with an expensive electronic lock. This is the makeshift lab where Gaines fabricated the pathogen.

When the terrorists realize they're busted, they check to see if their avenues of escape are cut off. If not, they attempt to flee, running separately into the surrounding woods and attempting to make it to the roadway. None run for their vehicles, since it would be too easy to cut them off if they tried to get away by car.

If escape seems unlikely, they stand and fight, using their super powers. Although trained by Davenport in close combat, none of them are experienced fighters.

Either way, they come pouring out of the headquarters building bearing assault rifles and, in small backpacks, one container apiece of the pathogen. These pose no danger in an outdoor environment, especially with the winds gusting ever faster.

Except for Patricia, all of the MRV members present are already wearing their black coveralls, as if preparing for an imminent mission. They don't bother to put on their masks or goggles before attempting to fight or flee.

As in "Super Siege", visual descriptions of the perps are given here, with personality notes in a follow-up section.

PATRICIA GAINES

Athletics 2, Health 2, Scuffling 2, Shooting 6

Powers: Entangling Hair 10, Wall Crawling 10, Webbing 10

Weapon: assault rifle +1

ALVIN DUNNING

A somewhat obese young African-American man who has shaved his head and wears a pair of thick-framed eyeglasses, complete with elastic band to keep them in place.

Athletics 6, Health 6, Scuffling 6, Shooting 2

Powers: Lightning Decisions 3, Psionic Blast 18, Threat Calculus 3

Weapon: assault rifle +1

JOEL BAILEY

A young Caucasian man, nondescript aside from his 70s-style sideburns and long dark hair, which he wears tied into a ponytail.

Athletics 2, Health 2, Scuffling 2, Shooting 6

Powers: Natural Weaponry (claws) 18

Weapon: assault rifle +1

HARD HELIX

JEFFERY MILAN

As described on p. 71.

Athletics 4, Health 10, Scuffling 2, Shooting 6

Powers: Fangs 8, Disease Immunity 48

Weapon: assault rifle +1, fangs 0

NORA ROUNDY

A rail-thin young Caucasian woman, freckled and red-headed.

Athletics 2, Health 2, Scuffling 2, Shooting 6

Powers: Empathy 4, Nondescript 8, Observe Dreams 8

Weapon: assault rifle +1

The scene probably ends in the apprehension of the suspects.

If any escape, they go on the lam separately. You may elect to play out their pursuit and capture in an improvised sequence, or allow them to be nabbed off-camera in other jurisdictions, in response to an APB filed by detectives.

In either case, the detectives are now free to examine the scene for evidence.

Found in the main building is a micro-laptop containing a Power Point presentation, a digital projector, and a screen. The presentation lays out a plan for Dunning, Bailey and Roundy to conduct a suicide attack on a local historical site, unleashing the bioweapon in an enclosed space. The attack was planned for the very next day. A second presentation provides plans for recruitment in the wake of their presumed deaths. It mentions Gaines and Milan as providing support. **Textual Analysis** suggests that references to another figure, the leader and probably author of the presentation text, have been edited out.

A 1-point **Chemistry** test, if performed on the shack before it is entered, detects inactive traces of the killer pathogen. Protocol requires hazmat suits be used by anyone entering. **Chemistry** finds that its crude assortment of lab equipment would be sufficient for production of the pathogen, given a starter supply of USR. Notes found on the laptop show that the group's USR supply has been depleted. One folder contains preliminary plans to raid Sussman's lab for more. Detectives can now consider themselves to have found and secured the source of the bioweapon.

A further 1-point **Chemistry** spend notices a few disused beakers and burners, along with residue suggesting that the shack was used for another purpose before it was converted to pathogen production: this used to be a meth lab.

(core) A few hundred meters from the two buildings, detectives discover a home grown gun range. Heavily perforated paper targets, bearing military-style human silhouette designs, have been affixed to bales of hay. (More paper targets are found, still in their packing materials, in the larger headquarters building.) Piles of spent rifle and pistol shells and casings lie strewn throughout the area. A **Ballistics** test on the many bullets found here finds matches to all of the weapons found during this sequence and Super Siege. Among the sources of shells and casings, a single gun remains unaccounted for: a .45 magnum revolver. When this ballistics pattern is run through the system, it comes up as a match for two unsolved crimes:

- The wounding of meth dealer Jasper Lebron, three years ago.

- The murder of radio show host and mutant activist Mark Hein, two years ago.

RINGLEADER
SCENE TYPE: CORE

Surviving suspects from the quarry apprehension are, if anything, even more close-mouthed than any counterparts captured during "Super Siege." They admit to being MRV members and promise that they are only the beginning of a wave of destruction that will put the norms in their place once and for all. They uniformly refuse to spill the identity of their ringleader.

Background checks reveal the following about the additional suspects detectives found at the scene:

- Alvin Dunning's high intelligence and low social awareness left him an outcast in his rough neighborhood. His regretful mother, Tamekia, wishes he would get back in touch with her. Alvin qualified for a university scholarship but dropped out of sight after getting into a quarrel with his high school guidance counselor and damaging his brain with a psionic blast.

- Joel Bailey's father Kenneth is a wealthy divorce lawyer who struggled with his son's lack of interest in fulfilling his potential. When pressed, Kenneth concedes that he may have frozen his son out emotionally when his mutant powers came to the fore.

- Nora Roundy, a natural middle child in a huge clan of foster kids and adoptees, never fully adjusted to the stresses of a large family, admits her mother, Alicia Roundy.

The lead detective in charge of the still-open Mark Hein murder is Margo Carmona. Hein was ambushed on his way to a book signing in the downtown core. A fiery mutant-rights proponent, Hein was the constant recipient of death threats, presumably from members of the barhead movement. She knew of the ballistic connection to the Lebron case but was never able to make anything of it. Carmona still likes Davenport for the murder but never turned up enough evidence for a search warrant.

The investigating officer in the Jasper Lebron case is a Detective Glenn Roberts. Before his lieutenant ordered him to kick the stagnant case to the inactive drawer, he had narrowed his list of suspects to three of Lebron's criminal associates: Brian Luther, Nelson "Donkey" Henrickson, and Russ Davenport. Luther and Henrickson were, he suspected, producing the crystal meth that Lebron and others sold, with Davenport as their enforcer. All four men had white supremacist connections; Davenport was also a heavy-duty barhead. Roberts was unable to make progress in the case, based on the victim's refusal to cooperate. Lebron is now serving a ten year sentence for drug trafficking.

Jasper Lebron may be a low-life drug dealer, but is appalled as anyone by the murder rampage of the MRV. If approached with a mix of **Flattery** (acting as if it goes without saying that he's enough of a citizen to cooperate against terrorists) and **Negotiation** (offering a sentence reduction and protective custody against barhead inmates) he agrees to testify that Davenport shot him with his beloved .45, which he called "Old Salty."

Research also shows that Davenport was exonerated of sexual assault eighteen months ago, after a DNA sample he provided failed to match the rape kit evidence. A look at his DNA test result using **Forensic Anthropology** shows that he is not a mutant.

If interviewed before they put all this information together, the detectives find Davenport to be a calm, subtly smirking witness. Claiming to be simply a regular Joe who makes an okay living as a motorcycle customizer, he categorically denies any connection to anti- or pro-mutant terrorism.

Any of his terror dupes, shown a photo of Davenport plus the evidence of his barhead past and non-mutant status, reels in shock. After struggling to assimilate the fact that they've used to further the enemy's agenda, the witness confirms Davenport as their leader.

This identification gives the detectives what they need to arrest him. Davenport offers up no resistance. He starts any interrogation by denying everything. Inside, he's dying to take credit for his genius plan. Goaded sufficiently by the mutant cops he hates, he proudly admits to doing what was necessary to touch off the inevitable race war—which the pure humans, outnumbering mutants a hundred to one, can't help but win.

WRAP-UP
SCENE TYPE: DENOUEMENT

In the days that follow the announcement of Davenport's arrest, public opinion shifts. People are still afraid of mutants, but now view the barheads with equal revulsion. Public pressure mounts to crack down on anti-mutant forces.

The detective who got ambushed on the Jim Hutchins show is invited back, to be celebrated as a hero.

If you played up the feds as major obstacles, they are forced to eat crow. They admit that the local cops did what they couldn't.

Squad members are commended for their efforts. If one of them showed particular political skill, he is told through back channels that the brass has an eye on him when future promotions come up.

HARD HELIX

⚛ CHARACTER QUICK REFERENCE

Bonnie Kreger - demanding middle-aged lady, mother of Gerry

Gerry Kreger - beating victim

Romeo "the Mule" Olivieri - restaurant owner with mob connections

Lt. Ken Swailes – Police tactical team leader

Jayson "Hiroshima" Chee – MRV member, radiation projector

Mary "H2O" Delozier – MRV member, Water manipulation

Ferdinand "Icewing" Licata – MRV member,

Billy "Blood Bug" Moran, MRV member

Josie "Tunguska" Pearl – MRV member, Heat Blast

Simon and Melba Chee – parents of Jayson Chee

Catherine Semple – Mother of Mary Delozier

Eugenio Licata - famed automotive engineer, father of Ferdinand Licata

Joseph Pearl and Marie White Cloud – parents of Josie Pearl

S.A. Allen Sanford – Federal agent

S.A. Gloria Stefaniuk – Federal Agent

Jim Hutchins – host of The Big Bulletin TV Show

Jeffrey Milan – MRV member, Disease Immunity, Fangs

Giselle Clauson – Production assistant at the Big Bulletin

Rocky Riele – former classmate of Jeffrey Milan

Bernice Hollings – former foster-mother of Jeffrey Milan

Dan Haskin – former roommate of Jeffrey Milan

Sharon Bryson - Genetic Action Front leader

Dr. Trina Ward – head of the Biotech Department at the local science university

Dr. David Sussman – research biochemist

Patricia Gaines, MEV member

Madhura Rawal, Lab tech., co-worker of Patricia Gaines

Yvette Boykins – neighborhood busy-body

Alvin Dunning – MRV member, Psionic Blast

Joel Bailey – MRV member, claws

Nora Roundy – nondescript MRV member

(Jasper Lebron) – incarcerated Meth Dealer

(Mark Hein) murdered radio show host and mutant activist

Tamekia Dunning – Mother of Alvin Dunning

Kenneth Bailey - Joel Bailey's father

Alicia Roundy – Mother of Nora Roundy

Det. Margo Carmona – lead detective in the Mark Hein murder case

Det. Glenn Roberts - investigating officer in the Jasper Lebron case

(Brian Luther, Nelson "Donkey" Henrickson) – suspected Meth. Cookers

Russ Davenport – barhead, leader of the MRV

INVESTIGATIVE ABILITY CHECKLIST

This table shows the sum of the clues available for each ability in each adventure, with core clues marked by grey cells. During character generation you can use the table to make sure that the PCs cover the necessary abilities, preferably with some redundancy for core clues.

INVESTIGATIVE ABILITIES	HARD HELIX	THE VANISHERS	SUPER SQUAD	CELL DIVISION
Anamorphology	4	2		3
Anthropology	1			
Architecture			1	1
Ballistics	3			1
Bullshit Detector	6	2	12	2
Bureaucracy		1	3	
Chemistry		1		8
Cop Talk	1	2	6	1
Data Retrieval	2		6	3
Document Analysis		1		1
Electronic Surveillance				5
Energy Residue Analysis			3	
Evidence Collection	3		2	4
Explosive Devices		4		
Fingerprinting	1			1
Flattery	5			1
Flirting	4		1	
Forensic Accounting		2	2	1
Forensic Anthropology	4		2	2
Forensic Pathology		1		
Forensic Psychology	3	2	4	4
History	1			
Impersonate	1			
Influence Detection				1
Interrogation	1	2		
Intimidation	5		5	
Law		3	3	1
Natural History			2	
Negotiation	4	4	5	1
Reassurance	6	1	3	2
Research		6	4	6	7
Streetwise		5	8	2
Textual Analysis				1
Trivia	3	1	2	3
TOTAL	64	38	76	56